FORGIVENESS ACTION IN

CAROL L. CURTIS

TATE PUBLISHING
AND ENTERPRISES, LLC

Published by Tate Publishing & Enterprises, LLC
127 E. Trade Center Terrace | Mustang, Oklahoma 73064 USA
1.888.361.9473 | www.tatepublishing.com

Tate Publishing is committed to excellence in the publishing industry. The company reflects the philosophy established by the founders, based on Psalm 68:11,
"The Lord gave the word and great was the company of those who published it."

Book design copyright © 2014 by Tate Publishing, LLC. All rights reserved.
Cover design by Rodrigo Adolfo
Interior design by Joana Quilantang

Published in the United States of America

ISBN: 978-1-63063-915-0
1. Fiction / Romance / General
2. Fiction / Romance / Contemporary
14.03.10

DEDICATION

This first book I would like to dedicate to Joan Curtis and Derek Feuerhelm for their support and encouragement, to both of you I extend a heartfelt thank you.

CHAPTER 1

Charity's wandering eyes quickly found their intended target, that tall handsome cowboy standing in the middle of the corral surrounded by the horses they had just purchased. Charity and the other ranch hands had already seen him at work and knew how patient he could be. Did no one except her see the sorrow he tried to hide when he gave his dimpled smile that didn't quite reach his sky blue eyes? Charity couldn't help but wonder what had happened in Daniel's life to give him that look. Immediately after the thought came the realization that Charity could see it. *Why Lord, is it because I need healing myself?*

Muttering to her coffee cup Charity stated, "It just isn't fair what that man can do to a pair of jeans. How can I get any work done when I have the image of a certain tall dark and handsome cowboy in my head?" Immediately after came another thought provoking question "What if my needing a Foreman had nothing to do with why the Lord sent Daniel here? Here I am questioning what

I ever did to have attained Daniel as my Foreman when the truth could possibly be, maybe the Lord sent Daniel here to be healed."

Charity forces herself to stop gazing at Daniel and get back to updating the accounts. Running the Dude Ranch was all she could handle (for the moment). No time for wishing life had turned out differently and that the handsome cowboy out there would carry her off on his majestic steed. *Where did that come from?*

Charity got up too quickly and her legs folded. "Why did this happen, God?" she cried out as she picked herself up. No answer came, as always.

Just then, Daniel opens the back door, "Are you alright?" *How does he seem to know when I am hurting?*

She composed herself right away. "Yes, I just got up too quickly. I sometimes forget that I am not as I used to be!"

Three years ago, Charity's life changed in a moment. Her parents and brother died that day, and she ended up in a coma for months—all because of a drunken driver.

Then her memories began to enfold her…

CHAPTER 2

Charity was so excited. She had a date with Jimmy! She hung up the phone and ran to tell her mother. "Mom," she shouted. "Jimmy just called and wants take me out, he said he would be here at six-thirty. What shall I wear?"

Faith looked up from baking the pies for the church social. "Why not that pretty blue dress we got last month? You haven't worn it yet."

Charity hugged her mom. "Oh, Mom! That's perfect! I had forgotten all about that dress! Thanks Mom." Faith could see the excitement in her daughter's face.

Charity ran out to the stable and yelled out. "Dad, Jess! Guess what? Jimmy just asked me out!" She slowed down as she approached the last stall where they were tending the newest addition to the stables Sarah, right next to her stall was her mom, Sugar who insisted on hanging her head over the rails just to make sure things were okay.

At two months old Sarah had cut herself deeply on a wire fence so they were keeping a close watch on her recovery. Charity reached over the fence and stroked her head. "How are you today, Sarah?"

She nickered and went straight for Charity's pocket where she usually carried an apple or a sugar cube for her. However, today she was just so excited about Jimmy asking her out that she had forgotten to grab something as she ran out of the house. "Sorry, Sarah. Not today." Her father and Jess both looked at her, thinking that this has to be something big if she forgot her horse.

"So, Charity". Her dad stood up and crossed his arms on his chest, "How come Jimmy didn't ask me first?"

"Dad!" Charity's cheek started to lightly blush as she responded "It's not like he's going to ask me to marry him!" Once her face was back to its normal color her father continued on with

"Doesn't matter, Charity. You tell him he needs to talk to me first!" as he was wagging his finger in the air at her. Charity couldn't help it she burst out laughing. "Oh Dad that was just so funny, you know that has never worked on me." She looked away for a second to swallow the next set of chuckles before turning to face her father. "I'm sorry Dad, you're right, I need to do it your way. Can I call him from the stable office?" He unfolds his arms as he walks toward her, "Now that wasn't so bad was it honey?" She shook her head " No, it wasn't and thanks for the gentle reminder Dad." Her father hugged her before she left to head to the office.

Charity looked at Sugar and stroked her once more. "I'll be right back," she whispered.

Off she went dashing to the stable office, grabbing the receiver she quickly dialed Jimmy's number and explained what her dad had said. "Sure, Charity. No problem," Charity hollered out to the stable. "Okay Dad, Jimmy's on the phone now." Chris Stewart walked in and took the phone from her.

"Thanks honey," Charity leaned in to hug her dad. "Hello Jimmy"

"Hello Mr. Stewart, I apologize. I should have spoken with you first but would you mind if I take your daughter out tonight?" Jimmy asked

"Well Jimmy, that all depends on where you plan to go."

"I was thinking of escorting her to the pie social, sir."

"Then yes, Jimmy, you may!"

Charity jumped up and hugged her Dad. "Thank you Dad you are the greatest."

"Okay now I should go see if Mom needs any help and ask if she can help me get ready later."

As Charity headed over to the house; Chris returned to the stall where he had left Jess with Sarah grumbling about women under his breath, Sugar (his horse) must have heard his voice, her head popped out of her stall in the hopes to be petted.

"Charity sure does spoil these girls" as he was petting her. Once Chris opened the gate on Sarah's stall Sugar's head was already back over the rails on the other side watching them, "Get it all settled then? Jess asks, "Yeah for now, I hope". Chris shrugged his shoulders in a (what can I really do) kind of shrug. Jess is still chuckling when Chris looks over at him serious all of a sudden, "Don't forget that this will be you if anything ever happens to me so watch closely and learn my friend." That sobered Jess up quickly, "Make sure that never happens, that child is a handful." Jess walked away muttering about families and kids, "I left home to get away from that!" Then he stopped dead in his tracks as he realized (I've made a new home and family here and now I'm thinking that family isn't so bad after all I like being a part of family.) Jess headed back to the stall he had just left, once back in he looked Chris directly in the eye, "I already consider you my family, I'm just saying the girl is a handful." They shook hands and Chris chuckled, "On that my dear friend we can agree."

As she ran into the kitchen, Faith yelled out. "Slow down, young lady. Unless there's a fire."

Charity laughed. "Oh, Mom! Of course there's no fire, I'm just so excited!" she exclaimed. "Can I help you with anything?"

"Not right now, sweetie. Do you want me to help you get ready?"

"Only if you'll have enough time to get yourself ready."

"I wouldn't miss this for a month of Sunday's sweetie. It sounds as though you really like this boy."

"Oh, Mom! He is so cute!"

Charity grabbed an apple off the kitchen table sliced it up and went right back out to the barn. A promise was a promise.

She spent the rest of the afternoon in her room until she heard her mom ring the dinner bell. She came running down the stairs as her dad and Stephen were coming in from the barn. She was just at the last couple of steps when Stephen glanced up, "I hear you got a hot date tonight, sis." Stephen then turns towards his father.

"Do you think I should hang close by them and be the chaperone?"

"That won't be necessary, Stephen. Your mother and I will be there."

"Cool, Dad. I was hoping you would say that." Then he grinned and ran up the stairs to wash up. Chris and Faith both just shook their heads and stated I'm sure glad we only had two kids.

After dinner Charity rushed through the dishes, thankfully she only had to wash. She came up the stairs and called out, "Mom, I'm taking a shower!" After her shower, her mother knocked on the door. "Are you ready for some help now Charity?" "Yes Mom." They had a good mother daughter time. At twenty past six, she walked downstairs eager for Jimmy to arrive.

She heard a cat call from her brother.

Her Dad just smiled, and said, "Honey you look beautiful."

A few minutes later the doorbell rang and Charity jumped up but her dad waved her back. "I'll get it honey!"

Since Jimmy wasn't expecting Mr. Stewart to answer the door, he gulped.

"Good evening, sir. Is…uh…Charity ready?"

Charity walked up to the door and her dad moved away. When Jimmy saw her standing there, he said, "Wow! You look beautiful."

She blushed. "Thank you. Are you ready?"

"Yes."

As they got to his truck, instead of going around to her side, he simply let her get in by herself. Looking from the window Mr. Stewart just shook his head. "Things sure are different then when I was a young man."

Faith looked up. "Why?"

"He didn't even open her door!"

"Well dear, some men just don't learn."

"Are you ready to go, honey?" Faith asked her husband.

"Is Stephen driving himself?"

"Yes he's going to meet up with his friends from school I think."

"Okay then let me just grab the pies and we'll go."

From that point on, Jimmy and Charity was a couple. They would go out every Friday night and some Saturday nights, and they would sit together at church. Mr. Stewart did not want her going out every day. Charity and Jimmy liked going to a quiet meadow by the lake to just sit and talk, have a picnic, watch the lake and the activities, it became their "special place."

CHAPTER 3

Stephen and Amy were dating. Charity thought they looked like a perfect couple. He was so handsome and tall, and she was petite and gorgeous. Charity would dream of the day that she became her sister. They went everywhere together. They had such a glow about them, you would know they were in love just be looking at them. Stephen would go into town and stay for hours at the diner while she worked. Charity hoped that she and Jimmy would be the same way. Although as the summer progressed, she noticed a difference in them.

Stephen started spending more time with his friends. When she would stop in the diner with her friends, Amy seemed sad. She wanted to ask her brother what was the matter, but didn't. *I hope that it is just a lover's quarrel*, she thought. After a couple more weeks, she overheard him talking on the phone with another girl. Then she knew something had happened. She even talked to Jimmy about it, but he had no idea why they had cooled either.

Stephen went around the house mad at everyone for at least a month. Dad finally ordered him out to the barn to have a talk with him. After the talk with Dad, Stephen was nicer to the family, but he never went out with Amy anymore. He didn't date much at all either—he seemed to withdraw. Finally, Charity couldn't take it anymore. She approached her brother and straight out asked him "Why are you so surly Stephen, what is going on between you and Amy? Whenever we run into each other in town she just looks so sad. What did you do?"

"Do I ask you about Jimmy and what you two do? This is something that Amy and I need to work out," Stephen snapped back.

"Okay, Stephen. Thank you for the honest answer, I will never ask you again."

"Thanks, Charity. I just need some time."

He hung out with his friends for the rest of the summer. Charity went on with her life and wondered what had gone wrong.

When summer was over Stephen, started working on the ranch as one of the hands.

He wanted to learn the family business from the bottom up. He spent a lot of time with his father, asking questions, and even took a course on ranching at the community college. Stephen and Nathaniel seemed to hang out a lot that year. One day in town, she overheard some guys at the diner talking about Stephen and Nathaniel will be hosting a raging party at the lake. Charity knew her parents wouldn't approve, so when she returned home she went to the barn to talk to her father. Jess was there but not her dad, so she told Jess what she had overheard and asked his advice instead.

"What shall I do?"

Jess put his hands on her shoulder. "I will talk to Stephen if you want me to. Your dad's out in the south pasture repairing fences today and won't be in until late."

"Would you please Jess, I don't want anything to happen to him."

Jess caught up with Stephen and spoke with him but to no avail; he went to the party anyway.

Stephen and Jess weren't talking much that year; he resented him for trying to tell him what to do. Even his dad noticed it. One day he told Stephen not to make any plans for that night, he wanted to talk to him in the study.

"Okay, dad. Whatever."

Chris Stewart looked at his son and remarked, "That attitude right son, there is the reason we need to have a talk."

That night Charity heard loud voices coming from the study. Her mother was there and comforted her.

"Charity this is between them. Stephen is becoming a man, and sometimes it is hard for a young man to follow his father's advice. Just pray for understanding and wisdom for both your Dad and Stephen, that is all we can do."

Stephen seemed to change after that evening. He quit hanging out with Nathaniel and spent more time at the ranch once again. Stephen didn't date for the rest of the year, and it seemed as if he wasn't even interested in girls. All he did was spend time with his friends.

Charity was now a senior in high school, she knew the prom would be coming up soon and had already talked to the principal to get permission for Jimmy to be her date. Jimmy had graduated two years prior, and it was school policy that a non-student could not attend any school activities without it. Once she got it though, she waited to tell him about it until he had actually asked her. Jimmy knew all about the school policy, so about a month before the prom he asked her if she wanted to attend and if she would get permission from the principal.

"Yes!" she answered. "And I've already talked to the principal. He gave permission for you to be my date."

"Perfect!" he responded. Charity told him, "Now that it's official I'll ask mom if we can go this weekend to look at dresses."

It was eight thirty in the evening when she got home that night, so excited. She ran into the living room to ask her mom if they could go shopping the next day. However, when she walked in her mother was crying.

"Mom what's wrong? Why are you crying?"

Faith looked up. "Stephen just announced that he wanted to join the service," she cried and buried her face in her daughter's arms. "He stopped in at the recruiter's office in town today and talked to him about it. Then he came home and talked to your Dad. Charity, I do not want him to go."

"Mom, Stephen's now a man. You have to let him make his own decisions."

Faith looked up again and said, "Your father told me the same thing but it still doesn't help. I still see you both as my little babies."

They were silent for a few minutes, and she began to calm down. "Oh well. I guess I shouldn't worry about it right now. He said it wouldn't be for a few more months anyway. He and Dad went out for a ride to talk more so I wouldn't be upset." She took a deep breath and smiled before changing the topic. "Now honey, what is it that has you so excited that you were running in my house?"

"Oh, Mom! Jimmy asked me to the prom. I was going to ask if we could go shopping for a dress tomorrow so I can tell him what color to wear"

"Of course we can, honey. I would love to."

They hugged and Charity said, "Mom, I love you and everything will be alright."

"Thank you honey, just please don't grow up anymore."

After hugging again, Charity whispered in her ear, "Mom I already have. Sorry." They pulled apart, and Faith tried to smile.

The next morning no one spoke about Stephen's decision but her dad did mention that last night he thought he had heard something about his two favorite girls were leaving him to go shopping today.

Charity smiled, flipped her hair back and saucily replied, "That would be me and mom." They all laughed, the air was lighter after that.

Shopping for a prom dress with mom turned out to be a fun day. They drove into town and after looking at a few dresses, Charity made her choice. She chose a floor-length, spaghetti-strapped red dress with an empire waist and white lace overlay on the top.

Faith got tears in her eyes. "Honey, I can't see how you could be any more beautiful than just now. I'm telling you right here and now that I'll be a basket case when we go shopping for your wedding dress," she exclaimed.

Charity rushed over to her. "Mom, thank you." She glanced at the sales clerk. "Wrap it up, please. This is the one we want."

After paying for it, they decided to stop in at the diner for a late lunch. As they walked in, Amy shouted from the back of the diner.

"Just find a booth, and I'll be right with you."

They both ordered soup and a half a sandwich. When their order was ready, Amy served them and asked, "So what's the special occasion?"

"We just came from getting Charity's prom dress," Mrs. Stewart said. She then proceeded to tell her about it, after they were through they paid the bill and headed home.

Charity couldn't contain her curiosity anymore, so she gave in and indulged. "Mom, can I ask you something?"

"Sure, honey. What is it?" (as Faith swerved a little to avoid hitting a rabbit).

"Why did Stephen break up with her?" (As that question sunk in Faith almost slammed on the brakes) Faith sighed. "He just wasn't sure about it, but I think it would have been fine given time, they could have worked things out."

"What things, Mom?" "Can we stop at the mail boxes mom? I'm waiting for a letter.

"Honey you remember when Amy moved here a couple of years ago?"

"Yes, but why?"

"Because her father kicked her out. She was pregnant."

"Pregnant? But she doesn't have a kid." Faith slowed down as they approached the collection of mailboxes for the homes strung along the country lane. Charity hopped out and back in quickly, "Nope, nothing yet. So finish telling me about Amy mom."

"She lost the baby," Faith replied. "And she was too proud to go back home, she hated her dad for kicking her out the way he did."

"Oh, Mom, I never knew." As they drove through the front gate of Stewart Ranch Charity was eager to hear the last of the story.

"Not too many people did, but she told Stephen and you know how he is about family."

"Yes, I do. You raised us to know that families are important that you need to forgive when they make mistakes."

"Yes, honey, that's correct. But she wasn't ready to forgive her father, so Stephen decided to just call it off until she changed her mind."

"Thank you, Mom. I'm glad you told me, I will add her to my prayers." Perfect timing she thought as the pulled up to the front of the house and Faith turned the car off.

That night after dinner and the dishes, Charity went upstairs to put on her dress to show her dad.

"Oh my! Are you sure that is not a wedding dress?"

Stephen just stared at him when he said that. "Are you crazy dad? They are all white."

"Chris looked over to him. "Not always, son."

Stephen had the grace to bow his head, he knew exactly what his father was getting at and since Charity knew about it now, so did everyone else in the room.

The month flew by. *Only one more week*, Charity thought. The night of the prom, she and her mom spent a couple of hours doing her hair and makeup. When she was ready, she walked down the stairs and her dad immediately began taking pictures. A few minutes later, Jimmy rang the doorbell.

This time Stephen answered the door and being the protective brother, warned her sister's date. "You and I went to school together, if you do anything to hurt my sister I'll come looking for you," he said, then he let him in.

Jimmy darted a look at him standing next to his dad and he got the message: *don't mess with her.* He pinned her corsage on and they left.

When Charity got home, they were all there waiting up for her.

"I just had the most perfect night of my whole life," she said. Then she turned and waltzed upstairs to get ready for bed to dream about Jimmy.

About an hour later, it dawned on her that all three were in the living room. *Oh well, I will ask mom in the morning,* she thought. However, she could not get to sleep and went downstairs to make some hot chocolate. To her surprise, Stephen was in the kitchen.

"What's up big bro? "Why aren't you asleep yet?"

He looked at her and said, "I've just been thinking."

"About what?" she asked.

"A lot of things."

"Anything you can tell me?"

"Yes, I told mom and dad what I had said to Jimmy when I answered the door."

"What did you say?"

"I told him that if he hurt you in any way that I would come looking for him."

"Why?" asked Charity.

Stephen looked her straight in the eyes, "Because Amy's date got her pregnant on her prom night."

Charity got up hugged her brother. "I've known since mom told me the day we went dress shopping about the reason why she moved here."

"Thank you Stephen."

"For what?" he asked.

"For loving me."

He smiled, hugged her again. "Your welcome, did Jimmy mention it?"

"No."

"That is why I stayed up, I figured if you were going to yell at me, I wanted mom and dad there."

"Coward."

He grinned. "Well now that I have confessed, I'm tired so I think I can go to sleep." They both cleaned up the kitchen and went to their rooms.

Unbeknownst to them their parents were still up and had overheard them talking they hugged each other and turned into their room as Faith said to Chris, "We must have done something right while raising them."

Stephen and Amy started seeing each other that year secretly. He didn't want anyone to find out yet, so they always meet at the lake and went to the next town over for their dates.

After that came graduation. Then one day in June, Stephen asked at breakfast if they would all sit down and stay because he had something to say.

"You all know I decided to join the service. Well, Amy and I have been dating quietly this summer. We have talked about everything. She recently had talked to her parents, so we decided that when I return, we would get married. I told her love you her but I want to wait until I return to set the date."

Everyone jumped up and starting talking all at once. Stephen stood up and exclaimed, "Okay calm down, everyone."

That got their attention, and they all sat back down then. He then proceeded with the rest of his news. "I am leaving in September. That will give us a couple of months together and while I am gone, Amy and I will be writing to each other. She would like to throw a party for me and wondered if she could have it here?"

Faith looked him directly in his eye and said, "Just try having it anywhere else and see how mad your mother can get."

Stephen laughed then. "Okay you and Amy can plan it out then."

Faith drove into town the next morning to the diner to have a long chat with her soon-to-be daughter-in-law. They both decided to invite the entire community to the party.

Faith hugged her. "Can I say welcome to the family now? And that it's about time my son realized what a special girl you are."

Amy blushed. "Thank you, Mom."

Faith could not help it—she broke out in tears of joy.

Sunday morning at church, they made the announcement about Stephen's departure and the party they were planning. When they got home after church, Faith went directly out to bunkhouse and told the crew of men that had stayed home to do the chores what she had announced in church.

"Is there anything we can do?" Simon asked.

She smiled and replied, "You bet!" She then proceeded with telling them the plans that she and Amy had come up with and they added some of their own ideas.

It was a week before the annual Fourth of July picnic. Faith asked Charity if she would help her bake the pies for the church's pie booth, and she quickly agreed. Spending time with her mother was one of her favorite things to do—that, and riding her horse, and spending time with Jimmy. It seemed that she was always on the go. Faith asked Simon if he needed anything before they headed off to the market. He gave her his list and they set off. This year, it was Faith's turn to make all the pies. She figured fifteen to twenty pies would bring in a lot of money for the church's missionary fund.

From the moment they entered the store they kept running into people they had to stop and visit with. After chatting with a few of the ladies Faith felt she had gotten enough confirmation that this year she should make a mixture of fruit and cream pies. Hopefully they would buy them all and prove she was making the right decision.

When they had gotten everything they needed, they headed to the checkout stand. Cindy was their clerk, so Faith asked after her father who was terminally ill.

Cindy looked up and sadly replied, "Things are rough right now. Dad isn't responding well to the medicine. Doc Jensen comes over a few days a week to monitor him."

"Well we are praying for him and the rest of your family, Cindy."

Since she was at work, she finished ringing them up and said, "Thank you for all your prayers."

That next week Faith and Charity spent a lot of time in the kitchen making the pies. You would have thought they were both teenagers the way they giggled and had so much fun together. Every now and then, Chris would walk into the kitchen and hear them together; he knew why he had fallen in love with Faith. She was the prettiest woman around, and she knew how to enjoy life.

Charity and Jimmy were still going out but lately she had noticed he had gone cold. So she asked him outright.

"Did I do anything wrong?"

"No," he said, holding her hands but avoiding her gaze. "I have just been working some overtime."

Nevertheless, Charity felt something was different but she accepted his answer, for the time being.

There were only ten days before the big farewell party for Stephen; things were getting busy around the ranch. There were tables that need scrubbing, bales of hay to scatter around for seats, table clothes that need ironing, more food needed to be prepared. BBQ racks were built for the smoking of the meat, everywhere in the yard and all things were being decorated. It was beginning to look like a party was going to happen there.

Two days before the party, Jimmy asked Charity to meet him at their special place at 7 p.m. After finishing the supper dishes, she told her parents.

"I'm going to meet Jimmy."

"Okay honey, drive safely."

When she arrived she thought, *this is it. I think he is going to ask me to marry him, why else would he have been working so much overtime this summer?* She got out of the car and walked to their spot, and she waited for half an hour for him. She finally spotted Jimmy, but to her surprise, Lucy had come also.

"Charity, I don't love you, we came here to tell you together, the day after Stephen's party we are running away to be married," Jimmy sheepishly said. "She's the reason why I kept telling you I was working overtime so much this past year."

Tears welled from her eyes. "Congratulations then I guess," she said in between controlled sobs. She turned and ran back to her car. She didn't want to go home just yet, so she went to the other side of the lake and cried her heart out.

When she was through crying, she went home and went directly up to her room. She didn't want to ruin the party, so she decided not to say anything until afterward. Saturday, Charity found it very hard to smile naturally, but she did try. It seemed to work because no one had asked her yet if something was wrong. Amy was staying over as they had last minute things to do, and Charity helped out only when they asked her.

Sunday morning dawned, such a beautiful day for a party. Slowly, she got up and got ready for church.

"Is there something wrong?" Stephen asked while they were having breakfast.

She turned towards him and responded, "I'm just sad you are leaving me today, big bro." He seemed to accept that, and she walked away. Charity thought it would be very uncomfortable going to church that day but Jimmy and Lucy didn't come. As they were driving home, the inevitable happened.

CHAPTER 4

It was Stephen's farewell party; he was heading off to active duty. The family and the community had made plans to send him off with a big party. Returning home from church that day, they were excited but sad too because it was it was Stephen's last day home. As usual, some of the ranch hands stayed home to do chores, but that day others had volunteered to stay home to start setting up the tables and get things ready, knowing that they would all get the chance to attend the second service before the party was to start. That was just the way life was on the ranch, everyone went to church. Her parents believed that faith in God was the most important thing in a person's life, and they lived it every day.

Stephen had invited all his buddies to come to the party. One of his friends, Nathaniel, had stopped off at the Quickie mart and picked up a case of beer; since there was still a couple of hours until Stephen's party started, he decided it wouldn't hurt if he started early, after all his best friend was leaving plus he knew there would be no alcohol there. Nathaniel couldn't quite accept that Stephen's whole family didn't drink and that they attended church regularly. His grandmother went, but he thought that was because she was just old. His parents had never thought it was that important, and they were not bad people.

Nathaniel drove out to the lake and drank his beer, when there was no more he got in his truck and headed to the Stewart's home. Racing down dirt roads was fun, and they did it all the time. This time, he did not bother to slow down as he turned onto the highway. He never saw the car until it was too late—it rolled over several times until it slammed into the bridge. That sobered him up somewhat so he called 911 to report the accident. The next thing he knew the police were taking him away. It was then that he recognized the car—Stephen's SUV—what had he done?

Charity knew immediately that she was hurt, but it was so quiet in the car. She wondered why she didn't hear any other noise. Then as she heard the sirens in the background, everything went black.

➤⁄↑↖

Months passed and Charity remained unconscious. One day she finally woke up. She turned to the nurse.

"What day is it?" she murmured.

"It's Wednesday," the nurse said.

"I've been here three days? Where is my family, are they alright?"

Sophia quickly turned away. "Let me go tell the doctor you are awake."

As she walked out of the room, Charity looked around to see if she could see why she was still in the hospital after three days. Her right leg was all mangled and scarred. *But this does not happen in three days,* she thought. *How long I have really been here.*

Just then, Sophia returned with the doctor. Doctor Luke Jensen had been her family doctor all her life; she knew he would answer her questions.

He walked up to her. "Welcome back little one, I've been wondering when you would decide it was time to wake up!"

"How long have I been here?" Charity quickly asked. "Where's my family, what happened to them?"

The doctor coughed and said, "Six months."

"S-s-six months? Are you kidding?" Charity sputtered out. "Where is my family? How are they?"

Doc Jensen looked away for a moment to compose himself—this was the hardest part of being a doctor for him. Nevertheless, he squared his shoulders and turned back to her to give her the answers that could possibly cause her to go back into another shock-induced coma. He took her hand in his.

"Charity, I have some bad news," he paused for a moment. "Both your parents and Stephen died upon impact. "Your leg was crushed and had gotten caught in the twisted metal of the car door and you've been in a coma the past six months."

Charity gasped and grabbed his arm. "No! No! No!" she screamed. "Why did you save me then? For what so I can live as a cripple and be all alone for the rest of my life? Please just get out of here. I don't want to see you right now!" As she turned away from both of them, she began to cry.

Sophia and Doctor Jensen stepped out into the hallway to give her a few moments. However, as a doctor and a nurse it was up to them to go back in.

Sophia hugged her and asked, "Charity, can I do anything for you? Can I pray with you?"

As Charity's tears were falling down her face, she turned away. "No!" she muttered. "And I don't need God anymore. He just took away everything in my life I've ever loved."

What could Sophia say to that? Nevertheless, friends never stop praying for friends and she didn't intend to do that. As she was walking out to see to her other patients, Sophia sent up a silent prayer asking God to intervene and restore Charity's faith.

Doc Jensen waited patiently through all of this then quietly told Charity, "When you're ready we can talk about physical therapy and rehabilitation for that leg of yours."

Then as he had other patients too, he turned to leave the room. As he did his heart broke for the little lost girl on the bed. Charity's heart hardened that day against God.

The next day Doc Jensen came to see her.

"Let's talk about physical therapy and rehabilitation now," Charity said

"Okay, I figure it'll take you about six months in all but I know that with all the prayers of the church members and your tenacity that you can learn to walk again," he said.

"I appreciate your assistance, Doc. But I don't want to hear about God right now."

He looked at her. "Okay, Charity for now I will concede. But that doesn't mean I will stop praying for you, and I'm not going to tell your friends and neighbors to stop either. Now back to the topic at hand. You'll need about six months of physical therapy."

"Six months? Why?" Charity squeaked out.

"Because you have been here for six months already and although we did exercises on your leg so it wouldn't suffer atrophy, it'll take some time for you to learn how to walk again."

She nodded her head as though what he had said made some sense. "Fine, but can I do that at home?"

"Well you could, not to be hurtful or anything, but you don't have anyone that can stay with you. I can make arrangements to have you admitted to the rehabilitation center just down the street from here."

"Alright but can I call Jess at least and tell him about the change in plans? I just called him yesterday after you and Sophia had been in to see me," Charity asked

Doc laughed. "Sure thing, Charity. It's not like I can make all the arrangements in the next hour!"

Charity called the house to let Jess know what the doctor was planning on doing.

"I was just going out to the truck to come see you when the phone rang."

"Oh please do come, I want to see you too."

When Jess arrived he was so happy that she was finally awake that he hugged her and started crying, so did Charity. Then Jess sat down and told Charity what they had done at the ranch during the six months while she was in a coma. He explained how they had all sat down to figure out how the ranch could continue to operate without the family to do the work.

"Simon and Todd had thought up the idea and we all voted on it."

She looked at him and after shuddering when Jess had mentioned her family. She straightened her resolve and said, "Okay so when are you going to tell me about it?"

"Hold on there missy, here goes, we decided to make it a working dude ranch," Jess started. Simon's the cook, and Todd keeps the books and he was the one to advertise to get people interested. Since he came from New York, he knew lots of people who would enjoy doing something like that."

Just thinking of all they had done to keep her ranch going she started crying.

"So far we have been booked solid. I hope you don't mind, Charity?"

She cried some more. "Come over here I want to hug you so I can show my gratitude," she said. Jess got up, came to her bedside and they hugged.

"I also had to hire a couple of guys, but they seem to fit right in with the rest of us. For now we all live in the bunkhouse," Jess continued. "It sure is good seeing it full again, since we only take in five to six people at a time, they use the rooms in the barn."

Charity was remorseful. "I'm sorry you had to give up your rooms, Jess."

He just smiled. "Like I said, it's nice to see the bunkhouse all full again."

"I don't know much about the finances since I've been here for the past six months. Is there enough money to build separate cabins for the clients? Do we take families or just men?"

"So far it has actually been mostly couples and they don't seem to mind sharing a room with another couple," Jess said. "To answer your question though, yes as far as I know I believe you could afford to build them cabins, even after having to hire a couple of experienced men. Our next group is all men, something about a bachelor party, so they won't mind bunking together."

They talked for a while longer and then just sat holding each other's hands. As far as she was concerned, Jess was all the family she had left. When it was time for him to leave, they hugged and cried some more.

"I'll never stop thanking God that he saved you," Jess said.

She looked down and muttered, "Jess you are all I have now but please let's not talk about God. How you can say that he loves me if he took my family away?"

"Charity, God does love you. Just give yourself some time and then you won't be mad any longer,"

Then he left to go back home. By the next week, all the arrangements were completed and Charity was going to the Rehabilitation center just down the street.

During his visits to her in the hospital Jess had also told her all about the accident and how Nathaniel had broken down and wept during the trail. He kept repeating how sorry he was for everything.

"Charity, God works in mysterious ways and everything happens for a purpose, Nathaniel went to prison where he joined a Bible study and gave his life to Christ. He now leads the prison's Bible study and is taking seminary classes online so that he could become a minister," Jess said.

Charity didn't want to hear it though, she was grieving and mad at both Nathaniel and God.

CHAPTER 5

Nancy was her physical therapist but she was also the pastor's wife. Being a small community they couldn't afford to pay him much so when they approached him to be their Pastor, they had prayed about it. They felt that since their daughters were married already, they could live more comfortably if Nancy returned to work as a physical therapist. Every day Nancy would come in to get her and off they went to the exercise room to get Charity back in shape and learn how to walk again. Gradually through all the pain, she went on, wondering all the time, why. What was there to live for?

Charity had told Nancy right away not to talk about God, but of course Nancy couldn't do that. God was such a major part of her life, and she knew that he was in Charity's life also even though she did not want to acknowledge it right now. She also knew that her parents had raised both Stephen and Charity to believe that faith in God was the most important part of their lives, even more than her parent's. She knew that many people felt the same way Charity was feeling after such a catastrophic tragedy in their lives.

Charity's friends and neighbors would come to visit at first, but she didn't want any visitors and she would politely send them away, except for Jess who came every other day. Jess would tell her what was going on at home, he tried to cheer her up and help her from being so mad at God. However, Charity didn't want to hear anything like that. Each night he would pray for Charity, in fact both Jess and Nancy had added Charity's name on the prayer chain at church. Even though Charity wasn't ready for her friends and neighbors to come and visit, they were all praying for her recovery and that her heart would soften and allow God back in her life.

After one month went by, her leg was gaining strength that first week her exercise time was spent in a tub of warm water doing leg exercises, everyday Charity would ask Nancy.

"When can I do something more? I want to make this recovery as fast as possible."

Nancy kept encouraging her every day saying, "Looking better."

The beginning of the second week she came in to get her.

"Are you ready? Today is the day!" Nancy asked.

"Yes, anything but the tub, I don't see how that is helping any," Charity responded.

Nancy laughed and off they went to the exercise room where Nancy wheeled her straight over to the weight machines.

At the end of the every session, Charity would wish she could just go back to the bath only, the weights were hard work. The next session Nancy took her to the weight machines again but afterwards she wheeled her over to the tub.

Oh that felt wonderful, Charity thought. By the end of the week, Charity was more comfortable with working out on the weight machines.

The next week as they entered the exercise room Charity watched as Nancy actually put weights on the machine, granted it was only two pounds but after the weight machine that day she was looking forward to the tub. For the rest of the week they stayed at two pounds, and it got easier.

As the third week started, Charity was expecting a change in the session. Nancy disappointed her though because they stayed at two pounds. Each day she was waiting to watch her add more weight but she never did, by the end of the week Charity decided to just ask Nancy why she hadn't added any weight.

Nancy responded with, "Because you can't push it too fast, you need to go at this slowly if not you can harm the progress we have made already."

The fourth week Charity did note that Nancy had bumped up the weight to four pounds. By the end of the session, Charity was looking forward to that hot bath again. Who would have thought by adding just two more pounds that it would wipe her out? After that, she told Nancy that she was glad that she knew what was best for her.

"If it had been up to me, I would have immediately started with ten pounds and probably would have done permanent damage to my leg," she told her once in a session. She promised she wouldn't ever question the work-out schedule again.

The next week, Nancy added in the parallel bars. She had her start with just standing up for a few minutes a day and once again, Charity was really looking forward to the hot tub part of the session. Who knew that just standing would be so exhausting? As Nancy added new exercises, the sessions continued to get longer.

The second month started and the only changes were longer sessions. The second week of the second month, Nancy increased the weights by another two pounds.

The next day she introduced the small exercise ball into the routine; she would lay Charity on it and made her push the ball to make it roll. By the end of that day's time Charity was really looking forward to tub portion of her session.

The first day of the third week of the second month Nancy left everything as is, but then the next day she added on another two pounds. Charity thought, *I'm only at eight pounds in the second month, how could I have been so optimistic to think that I could start at ten pounds?* She started with zero pounds and felt as weak as a new-born kitten.

The next day while at the parallel bars instead of having her just standing, Nancy changed the routine. "Try to take a step," she said.

Oh my just one step that should be easy, Charity thought to herself.

However, her leg didn't want to cooperate that day either and if she didn't have the bars to hang onto, she would have fallen. Once again, Charity was hoping that she would not stumble while working the parallel bars that day, but that wasn't to be the case.

On Friday while on the exercise ball, Nancy added a few more minutes saying that this would help Charity to make that first step easier as her legs got used to the movement. She had her doubts but refused to give voice to them this time.

At the beginning of the third month, five minutes were added to each of the exercises. Nancy was encouraging her daily about the progress she was making. Charity was taking five steps now at the parallel bars; she felt more comfortable doing so.

That second day the weights were bumped up to ten pounds. The third day Nancy introduced the bicycle into her routine. This should be easy, Charity thought. *I can do this!* Once more Charity was dumbfounded that she had trouble riding a bike, she could only last a few minutes, and she felt like she had run a 5K marathon. For the rest of that week nothing else changed. Charity was so glad that she only had to exercise five days a week.

The second week of the third month, Charity was expecting more changes she wanted to pick up the speed so she could go home. Nevertheless, no changes came until the last week of the month when Nancy made her walk the length of the parallel bars. Granted they were only the short ones in the room, but she was so excited when she accomplished it that week. She actually felt like she was making great progress.

All during the rehabilitation, Jess would come to visit and tell her what was going on with the new construction and what was happening at church.

Charity wanted her recovery to go faster. She hated being in a hospital and not being able to move around. She also wanted to see the results of the construction. More than that, she wanted to be with the only family she had left—Jess and all the ranch employees that she had known growing up all her life. She was proud of them for thinking up a way to keep the ranch going while she was in the hospital and now while she's at the rehabilitation center. In addition, she was very curious about the new hands because for some reason, Jess was not as forthcoming with information about them. Jess continued to give her updates on Nathaniel too via his grandmother, Mrs. Davis. She was not interested in that part though, so she would tune him out.

Then Jess would stop in midsentence and call out. "Charity, Charity!"

She would tune back in and reply, "Yes, Jess?"

"Okay I get it, you aren't ready to talk about him yet," he said.

Any mention of Nathaniel and she would cringe, just thinking about his actions and how it had changed her whole life.

The fourth month Nancy took her to the long parallel bars but with the addition of five pounds on the weights. Charity felt like she had made no progress at all. On the second day however, she did better and she was back to thinking.

I'm so glad I'm making progress, she thought. That didn't last long because Nancy had added five more minutes to each exercise and made her do both of the parallel bars the next day.

About once a week, Doc Jenson would come by and check up on Charity's progress. Today was the day for his visit.

"Have I progressed enough to be able to go home?" Charity asked.

"Not yet, although I am impressed with your progress," Doc Jenson said. "The next step is to walk the parallel bars while only hanging onto one bar."

Charity gulped. "One bar? Am I really ready for that?"

He smiled at her reassuringly. "Yes that is the next step, and yes I do think you are ready." Nancy did that very thing the next day. For the rest of that fourth month, nothing else changed.

As the fifth month began, Charity knew that things would be progressing fast from here on out. So far, she could only go halfway on the long parallel bars but she knew that if she wanted to go home, she would need to be able to walk them without having to hang on it at all.

I wonder what changes Nancy will make this month, she thought.

When Nancy arrived to get her, she said, "By the end of this month I expect you to be comfortable with all the exercises because starting your sixth month you will be walking to the exercise room all by yourself, of course I'll be walking right next to you."

"Nancy, I've been wondering," Charity spoke up. "Just how many patients do you have?"

"Four and all of you are at two-hour sessions now," she answered her.

"When I started I told them that is all I would take on at a time because I didn't want to start with a patient and then pass her onto someone else when my other patients had progressed to the two-hour mark in their sessions. Some therapists don't mind doing that but I believe you get a better response out of the patient if you start and finish with them."

"You're right, let's get this month started then so I can be one month closer to getting out of here and going home," Charity said.

It took her all month to learn how to walk the whole length of the long parallel bars. It was exhausting but she felt like she had accomplished something.

The beginning of the sixth month and hopefully her last, Charity cornered both Nancy and Doc Jensen at the same time and asked,

"What is it going to take for me to be able to leave here at the end of this month?"

"You need to be able to walk on your own with no assistance," Nancy replied.

"When you can do that without assistance then I'll write up the discharge papers immediately," Doc Jensen added.

"Okay then. I know what I need to do to go home so let's get to it!" Charity replied.

She proceeded to get up right then and walked out the door headed to the exercise room. After that day, Charity was walking the halls all the time. Even after her two-hour therapy session was over, she was that determined to leave. On the day that she was to be discharged, Jess came to drive her home. Charity could see that age was catching up to him, and he was slowing down. She loved him and wanted him to always be there for her. After all he had been working for her family since he was a young man.

CHAPTER 6

As they got to the spot where the accident had happened, Charity had to look away. She didn't want to see it. She wondered if it would it look the same. Yet nothing was the same, and it never would be—she knew that now. Coming home that day was so hard for her. She wanted so much for it all to have been a lie.

She wanted to see her parents sitting on the front porch swing reading their Bible and waiting for her. Nevertheless, they weren't there and the truth was she had to walk into that house all alone and that it would be so quiet and she didn't want to be there.

She turned toward Jess and pleaded. "Can you take me to the stable room instead? I can't stay here just yet."

Jess squirmed. "Sorry, Charity. No can do," he said. "I hired a guy to help me out, and he lives in there since the cabins you had us build are finished. I moved back into my old room and gave him the other. I'm grooming him to take over for me."

Charity sighed and stood up a little taller. "Okay then, let's go in."

Jess smiled. "That's my girl."

"Will you stay and have a cup of coffee with me then?" Charity asked. "I want to hear more about this guy you hired to replace you." Jess made a pot of coffee and they sat at the kitchen table.

"Are you planning on leaving me?" Charity blurted out.

"No that isn't my intention at all," Jess said softly. "I was hoping you would let me stay in the bunkhouse with Simon. I'm getting too old to do the things I used to do, that's why I thought I should train someone."

Later that day, she met Daniel and fell in love. Although she would never let him know that.

Charity had previously requested Jess to announce that dinner would be at 6 p.m. and to have all the men come up to the house so she could thank them all for what they had done. She spent the rest of the afternoon checking the freezer and pantry and preparing a meal for the men who had gone beyond their duties to keep the ranch going and even had made a profit while she was gone. Standing at the kitchen window, she saw the men walking up to the house, and she was anxious for some reason. She had found a roast in the freezer and added fresh vegetables from the garden.

I wonder who tended it all this time, she thought.

As they came in the kitchen door, they were met with the smells of roast beef, homemade biscuits, and something that those who were there before the accident remembered so well, homemade pies!

She sent them into the dining room where she had set the table she wanted everything to be perfect. Jess and

Charity brought the food into the dining room and all the men stood up.

"Time to join hands and bless this food and the hands that provided it and thank him for bringing her back home to us," Jess said.

Daniel watched the men's faces as they did what Jess had asked, the ones that were here before had closed their eyes and were nodding their heads.

He could see that Charity and her family had made quite an impression on them. Jess had already told him the stories of how it had been before and wished that he could have known them, they sounded like a loving family. Jess said grace and they all sat down to eat. When it was time for dessert, Charity began clearing off the table and several of the hands joined in, they made quick work of it.

As they all came back in carrying plates and silver-ware and a few pies, you could see the men's eager look on their faces.

"Who wants pie?" Charity asked.

Every single man responded eagerly with an "I do." From then on, Daniel knew exactly why.

As Charity began to settle in, she got restless; cooking just wasn't enough to keep her occupied. In addition, the friends and neighbors who did come to see her were just quick visits as they all had their own ranches to run.

After a few days she called Jess out in the barn.

"I'm bored! Is there anything I can do?"

"Well let me think on this. Are you sure?" Jess replied.

"Yes I'm sure but it can only be a sit down job for now," Charity responded.

"Okay as I said let me think on this".

Then he called out to Daniel to go find Todd. An hour later, Todd was in the stable office talking to Jess about Charity and her wanting to work.

"Would you like to get back to ranch work and let Miss Charity take over the accounts?" Jess asked Todd.

"Oh Yes!" he replied.

And so they continued talking for a while longer. It was decided that Todd would ask Miss Charity tonight at dinner if she would take over the accounts, mainly because he missed being out in the saddle with the rest of the ranch hands.

That night at dinner while they were having dessert Todd spoke up and asked her, Charity was so happy she got up too quickly to go hug Todd and it happened, her leg gave out and down she went. Every man at the table except those that were where she fell jumped out of their seats to help her up.

Daniel was the first one there.

"Do you want me to carry you or do you want to do it on your own?" he whispered as he picked her up

"On my own," she whispered back.

He gently lowered his arm.

"Go for it!"

She was so grateful of his consideration of her feelings; she gave him a huge smile and continued on her way to go hug Todd. Her smile just then had knocked him for a loop just as his heart had dropped a few hundred feet when she fell. He felt like he always wanted to be the one there to protect her.

Todd blushed when she hugged him.

"Are you alright?" he whispered as they hug.

"Yes, thank you." She then let go of him.

"Ah Miss Charity you didn't need to do that!" he exclaimed aloud.

They all watched as she slowly walked back to her chair and no one mentioned they noticed that she was limping. After desert was over, all the men gathered up the dishes and cleared off the table. She had allowed Jess to escort her to the kitchen, but she was determined to stand on her own two feet here at the ranch. She didn't want them to feel sorry for her. Daniel walked out the kitchen door after he had made sure she was okay.

I wish I were the one who has to escort her, he thought.

The next morning Todd arrived with the ledger books, he sat down and showed her what he had done and explained that Simon did the grocery shopping and had refused to give it up.

"Simon wants you to make your list and he would add it to his list."

Charity felt humbled by the fact that the men desired to watch out for her. However, she resolved to be more careful when they were around from then on because she was not going to allow them to treat her as an invalid.

"Why don't we do the books on a computer?" she asked Todd.

He blushed. "Because I don't own one."

She dialed the stable's number and asked Jess if he could drive her into town.

"Not today. I'm doing all the vaccinations but I can have Daniel take you," he replied.

"Alright then. Can you tell me when he is ready to go so I can be ready?"

"Sure thing. I'll go talk to him right now."

They hung up and Jess yells out to the corral. "Daniel, can you come in here for a moment?"

A few minutes later Daniel came in. "What do you need, Jess?"

Jesse then explained what Charity needed.

"Sure I can take her, when does she want to go?"

"Just to call up to the house and let her know that you can be ready whenever she is," Jess replied.

Daniel called her right then, and Charity answered it. "Hello Jess?"

"It's not Jess. This is Daniel and whenever you are ready, so am I," Daniel replied.

"Anytime, because I'm ready now," she answered back.

"I'll just grab the keys and I'll meet you at the front door in a few minutes then."

He got as close to the front door as possible and got out to assist her down the steps, and she was waiting for him at the front door. He helped her into the truck and as he walked around to his side, Charity smiled just watching him.

"Where are we going?" he asked when he got in and headed out of the driveway.

"To get us a laptop and some type of accounting software CD," she replied.

"Good idea! That way Jess can just hand you all his records and you can enter them and keep an eye on things around here for yourself."

Then they just talked about things in general until they arrived at the store. Then he got out and came to her side to open her door and help her out.

"That's not necessary, you know."

"Yes it is. My mother raised me that way. A gentleman always opens and closes the door for a lady."

"But I am your boss."

"Ah…but you're still a woman."

When they finished there, Daniel turned to her.

"Are you hungry? I know I sure am."

"Yes. As a matter of fact, I am."

They stopped in at the diner for some lunch. Amy was working, when she saw Charity arrive with Daniel she smiled and waved to them, thinking WOW they make a cute looking couple.

They sat down in the closest booth and waited for Amy to come to the table. Within a few minutes, she came walking up with the menus.

"Want anything to drink while you are deciding?"

"What would you like, Charity?" Daniel asked.

"Ice tea please," she responded.

Amy went off to get their drinks.

"Are you ready to order or do you need a few more minutes?" Amy asked when she came back.

"I'm ready," they answered at the same time.

Amy took their order and then went on to her other customers who needed refills.

When their order was ready, Amy walked up to them and since they were talking to each other, she cleared her throat for them to realize that she was there with the food.

"Can I get you guys anything else?" she asked as she set down the food.

"No thank you," Charity replied.

Then it dawned on her she hadn't even give Daniel a chance to say anything. She sheepishly looked over at him and saw he was smiling and was relieved. Then she said Grace and as they started eating and thought, *oops, I did it again.* She looked up at him and if possible, he was smiling even more. *What a handsome man he is when he smiles.*

After lunch they headed back to the ranch, Charity was itching to get to work on converting the manual system over to a computer system. He got out of the truck, came around, and opened up her door. As he assisted her down, she thanked him for the enjoyable day. She was glad the salesperson had installed the software there so she could begin immediately.

After a short time of working on the computer, she realized she needed to start dinner. While it was cooking, she went back to the computer and resumed creating her accounts. It took her a week to get all the data entered. Once it was, she gave out a huge sigh. Y*es I am finally done!*

She decided to treat herself to an afternoon stroll in town, so she put supper in the crock-pot and called down to the stables to find someone to drive her.

It was Jess who answered. "I have some down time today. Are you ready now?"

"Yes I am!"

And so she and Jess spent the rest of the day in town.

At one point Jess asked her, "Can we stop by the church. I need to speak with the Pastor." Charity hesitantly agreed. When done in town, they returned home ready for another week on the ranch and chores. Jess had wanted to talk to Charity about retiring, but it just didn't seem as though it was the right time. *Someday soon though,* he thought.

The next week everyone was busy and the week just seemed to fly by. Sunday arrived and as the ranch hands were heading off to church, Jess stopped at the house to see if Charity would be going. He knocked and when she opened the door he had his answer, she wasn't going.

"We are leaving for church now do you need anything?" he told her.

"No, thank you. See you later," she replied.

As he drove into town, he prayed for her to be ready.

Charity had been home for a few months now and even though she went out to see her horse Sarah everyday and bring her an apple or a sugar cube, she wouldn't ride her. Jess wanted to talk to her about it but knew that when she was ready she would just do it.

Jess wondered at times. *Why is she afraid?*

Since the accident had happened, Amy hadn't visited her yet. It was long overdue.

When Charity opened her door and saw her, they hugged each other and started crying. Charity then apologized for not calling her when she had regained her conscientiousness, and Amy apologized for not calling or coming to visit her all this time. They ended up at the kitchen table having iced tea and cookies. Amy told Charity at first she was grieving but then decided she needed to get on with her life, after all no one but the Stewart's had known that Amy and Stephen were engaged, they had only known that they had started dating again that summer.

"I still think of you as my sister, but I am dating someone new now. I hope you don't mind," Amy said.

"No. Why would I mind, Amy?" Charity cried. "You are so beautiful! How could any man not want to be with you? Is it anyone I know?"

"No, after the accident I went home to my folks and grieved, during that time my father introduced me to Bruce. When it was time for me to return to work, Bruce decided to follow me. He works at the lumber mill on the other side of town. He asked me last night to marry him and I told him yes," she paused for a moment. "What I want to know is, will you still be my maid of honor?"

"Of course I will, but please tell me that you want us to wear floor length dresses because I don't want anyone looking at my legs."

Amy smiled and continued. "Stephen told me that summer that you knew why we had broken up. He also told me what he had said to Jimmy the night of your prom."

Charity winced when Amy mentioned him. Amy caught it though.

"Did something happen that night?"

"No Amy," Charity replied. "It happened two days before the accident."

"How did he hurt you, Charity? I know he did something by that wince when I mentioned his name."

"He…he…" she stammered. "H-he told me that he didn't love me. We met at our special place that night and he had brought Lucy with him. He told me that they were eloping the day after Stephen's farewell party."

Amy reached out and hugged her. "That snake isn't worth the ground you spit on. But I promise until you are ready, I will not speak a word about this."

"Thanks, Amy."

Thanksgiving is only a week away I need to do something about it, Charity thought. This would be her first one home since the accident. She went to Simon.

"I've invited Bruce and Amy to come celebrate Thanksgiving here. Would you like to prepare the meal this year? We will have it at the house as usual."

"I'd be honored to cook the meal but will you help me?" Simon replied.

Charity beamed. "That all depends on what help you want." Simon smiled. *At least some of the old Charity is still there.*

Thanksgiving morning arrived. As she woke up, she heard noises coming from the kitchen. She eagerly got up as she had done in past years to rush down to help her mom. When she opened the kitchen door, it was only Simon and not her mom standing there—her pain came back in full force.

She pondered, *why did you allow this Lord?*

However, she was determined to make this a happy day for everyone after all. She was thankful for all the ranch hands had done for her since the accident. That day turned out to be just as good as all the others had been for she had friends and her new family around her.

That got her to thinking about Christmas, so she decided to keep the family traditions going no matter what the circumstances. She went to Jess and asked if he would drive her into town on Monday morning because she needed to do some Christmas shopping and she needed to renew her driver's license.

Jess stared at her for a few minutes. "Of course!" he said. "And thank you for today, Charity. I know this was hard on you this year!"

Charity half smiled. ""You're welcome, Jess. And please keep reminding me to be more involved. I tend to withdraw into myself. I need to learn to get on with my life."

Jess just hugged her. "We all love you, Charity."

Monday morning as Charity waited for Jess to drive up to the house, she was making a mental list as to what to get everyone. She had waylaid Simon Saturday and had asked for ideas on what to get the men. This was the first year she had to worry about that kind of thing—normally that was her mother's job. She was feeling like she was finally an adult now with the responsibilities of running the ranch, being the owner and not just the child. Jess drove up just then. She grabbed her purse off the porch swing and walked down the steps and met him halfway.

"You always were the eager one," Jess said.

First thing she did in town was stop at the Department of Motor Vehicles (DMV) to renew her license. She walked out proudly, just as she had done the first time she had gotten her license.

Now off to the department store for Christmas shopping, she thought to herself. It took her awhile to choose the right things for each man and then she went to the women's section for Amy's gift. She wanted to find the perfect one but she didn't find it there, so she kept looking. Then she saw it—a beautiful shawl with gold and silver threads going all through it. She had purchased a book for Bruce; Amy had told her he liked poetry. She had found a wooden chess set for Simon and a wooden carving of a horse and her filly for Jess. The last person on her list was Daniel. She couldn't make up her mind on what to get him. She finally had narrowed it down to either a pair of soft leather gloves or a new horse blanket. She decided on the horse blanket because she knew how much he loved his horse.

All done, she thought. *I wonder where Jess went.* She looked at her watch and it was already two, they were supposed to have met up at the diner at one. She knew where he would be and then her stomach growled at her. *I guess I need to eat too!*

At the diner, she found Jess and Daniel in a booth chatting away while eating their food. As she approached the booth, Jess apologized for not waiting for her, but that Daniel had been there so he ate with him.

"Something came up that I need to take care, of Charity," Jess said. "So Daniel will drive you back after you eat." He paused for a moment. "Or you could drive him home!"

Daniel laughed. "Can I trust her driving?"

Charity smiled. "You won't know until you try."

Then all three laughed.

I like when she smiles, Daniel thought.

Charity liked driving but not for long, just driving home that day was enough for her for the time being. She noted Daniel wasn't hanging on for dear life so she knew that she was doing okay. Daniel on the other hand was fascinated watching Charity drive.

I wonder if she knows she keeps licking her lips, he said to himself. He sure wasn't going to be the one to bring it to her attention. But her lips did fascinate him.

It took Charity two days to wrap all the presents. She devoted a few hours each day to the task. In the meantime, she had gone up to the attic and brought down all the Christmas decorations. Now she was ready to go chop down a tree. She called the stables and asked Jess if he would like to go with her and select a tree.

"Sure thing! How about you give me an hour and I'll be ready to go."

"See you in an hour then, Jess."

As the truck drove up to the front, she noticed it wasn't Jess. As Daniel got out and they meet at the bottom of the steps he spoke up, "Jess decided he didn't want to go stomping through the snow so he asked me to come instead, I hope that doesn't bother you."

Once they returned from getting the tree, Charity walked out to the barn and asked Jess outright.

"Are you trying your hand at matchmaking?"

He chuckled. "Yes, I am," he said and walked off.

"Fine then, that's good to know," Charity sputtered and walked off herself.

It was Christmas Day. She got up to start making breakfast. As it was almost ready, the men started arriving. They sat down to eat after asking if she needed any help. She had invited Bruce and Amy but they had declined, they were going to her folk's house for Christmas Eve dinner and then his parents for Christmas Day. Afterwards they all dispersed to do the chores and then came back to watch the games because dinner would be at two. As the day progressed, Charity realized that having them all there was helping to ease her pain.

On New Year's Eve she went to Amy's. When she had invited her to come to her house, she told her, "It's just going to be a small gathering. I promise, Charity."

It was bigger than that though. She was actually surprised to see that Daniel was right by her side, as the clock struck twelve. He turned, grabbed her up in his arms, and kissed her.

"He kisses well, oh my!"

"Thank you," Daniel said shyly.

She blushed. She hadn't realized she said it out loud until it was too late.

Amy and Charity kept busy planning the wedding in the months to follow. She had Bruce and Amy over for dinner at least twice a month. She could see just how much Bruce loved her and hoped that one day a man would look at her like that.

Once Bruce took her aside and asked, "So you really don't mind that I'm marrying Amy?"

Charity smiled her biggest smile and exclaimed, "Not at all. I can see you love her and she deserves happiness."

Bruce just hugged her. "I hope I can measure up to your brother. She still talks about him, you know."

"She does?"

"Yes but I don't mind. I love her so much, I just hope in time that she will love me as much as she loved him."

"Don't fear Bruce. She does, I can see the joy and the happiness in her face, even when you aren't around.

"I hope you don't mind that we are still close."

"Not at all, Charity. You see, you are helping her to heal," he said and looked straight into her eyes. "So thank you."

Bruce had set the date of the wedding for September 1. That way both Amy and Charity would have something happy to think about on that day from then on. When Charity heard that she believed that Bruce truly was a blessing.

Charity didn't venture into town much that year except for the wedding plans. She still avoided going to church whenever asked. She did however, ask Jess to thank everyone for all the prayers. Healing was a slow process both physically and mentally for her.

Her birthday was coming up and both Amy and Bruce had approached Jess about having a party. She hasn't had a party since before the accident. Jess suggested they keep it small this year because of that same reason. May 20 came and unbeknownst to her, her party was at 7p.m. Bruce and Amy were bringing the cake in from town to keep it a surprise. All day she had been missing her mother, and no one had even mentioned it was her birthday so she was feeling sorry for herself.

When dinner was over the men declined dessert and headed back out to the barn. When the doorbell rang at seven, she wondered who it could be. As she opened the door, everyone was on the porch yelling.

"Happy birthday, Charity!"

She broke out in tears. "I thought no one had remembered. Come on in." She turned to Simon and Jess. "You rascals! I've been feeling sorry for myself all day long." That party was more precious to her than all the previous ones she'd ever had.

As the next three months flew by, Amy was getting anxious and nervous. Charity spent the night before the wedding at Amy's house after the rehearsal dinner.

When they arose, they immediately began getting Amy dressed. The wedding was at eleven thirty, so no food for either of them until the reception. Charity found that she was nervous too; this would be the first time she would enter the church since that fateful day two years ago. She was glad that Bruce had set the date for today though because this would surely help both of them heal. The closer it got to the time to enter the church though,

Charity considered backing out. She knew she wouldn't, but she wanted to. Daniel was Bruce's best man; that was one of the reasons she knew she wouldn't back out of it. She wanted to see him in a tuxedo. As she heard the music begin they entered the church, Charity glanced over to the left side front pew, squared up her shoulders and finished the walk down the aisle, all the while chanting to herself, "I can do this."

During the vows, Charity happened to glance over at Daniel and she just couldn't look away. She wanted to be the one up there saying the vows to him. *I'm in big trouble.*

➤⁄❘❮

Another year had passed, however Charity was still wasn't riding or attending Church. Jess finally decided he would confront her about it. He walked up to the house, knocked on the door and just walked in.

"Charity I need to speak with you."

"Sure, Jess. What about?"

"About you not doing what you used to do."

"What is that Jess?"

"You riding Sarah and going to church."

"No," she said.

"Why not?" he fired back.

She had the saddest look in her face. "Because riding and going to Church just remind me too much of Mom and Dad, and I'm still hurting." She exhaled deeply before speaking again. "It was so hard to walk down the aisle on Amy's wedding day, when I first entered I glanced at where they usually sat but I made it."

"Honey, you have to learn to forgive and live your life."

"Why?" What good am I now? I'm afraid to ride. What if I fall and can't get back on?" She paused again. "Church was Mom and Dad's second home. I can't go there and not see them there sitting in the front pew like always."

"Oh, honey," Jess replied. "I think I understand more now. When you are ready, can you promise me something?"

"What is that, Jess?"

"Come tell me right away just like you used to do?"

"I can do that Jess." She hugged him. "Thank you for being here, Jess."

"I love you just as if you were my own child, Charity."

CHAPTER 7

Daniel was in the corral when he felt compelled to go up to the house. As he walked in, the petite woman standing before him, just as it was on the day she came home from the hospital, struck him dumb.

Charity took his breath away. Sometimes he thought he actually forgot to breathe when he was around her. Her shoulder length cinnamon brown hair that was just the shade of his horse and those bright green eyes affected him everytime he saw her, too bad they looked sad most of the time. Daniel knew what it was like to bear a heavy burden. Five years ago, his wife—a wife he hadn't wanted in the first place—had died giving birth to their son, Josiah.

Josiah was living with Victoria's parents, for now. Josh and Vicki are good for Josiah but Daniel knew he would have to let go of his anger at God and raise his own son eventually, he just wasn't ready yet, or was he? He hadn't responded this way to a woman ever, not even Victoria.

When Daniel had found out Victoria was pregnant they eloped just so the town wouldn't know of his mistake, the one and only night of drinking in his life and look what happened, he had no self-control. He may not have loved his wife but from the moment he had held Josiah in his arms, he fell in love with him.

Charity smiled as he walked in. Who wouldn't if a good-looking single man with big bronze muscles walks in?

"Are you alright?" Daniel's concerned look made her blush but she managed a nod.

Where did that thought come from, Charity mused. *When did I become such a romantic?* As Charity smiled, Daniel's heart leapt and skipped a beat.

What is it about this woman, he wondered.

"Sit down, have a cup of coffee while I warm up breakfast," Charity said after a moment. "It'll just take a few minutes. Jess said something about you being in the south pasture earlier this morning and repairing a fence. After working so hard, a man deserves a hearty breakfast!"

Daniel didn't say anything so she went on chatting. "Was it the pasture that Brody is in? I know he isn't ready to be retired but he needs the rest just as much as Jess. They are both getting up in years and deserve to take it easy. Did you know that he was my Dad's wedding gift to mom?" Charity recognized that she was rambling and blamed it on Daniel's closeness (Why doesn't he step away so I can stop being so nervous)

Daniel smiled. "No, I didn't know that and no it wasn't. But you are right, he doesn't want to retire yet," he admitted. "Are you sure, you want to do that to him? You can let him stay in the corral so you could keep a closer eye on him but he needs exercise and no one has the time right now to do it. How about you doing it?" (The next step brought him even closer to her and he heard the tiny gasp as though she was having a hard time breathing.)

Charity squirmed. "No, I haven't ridden since the accident."

"Why not Charity?" As he reached up and tucked a stray strand of hair behind her ears

"Jess said Doc Jensen thought it would do you good."

"I'm just not ready," Charity whispered. Their eyes connected for a moment and time seemed to stop. Daniel decided he should be the one to take a few steps back and give them both a much needed break for now so he turned back to the table and took a seat.

Daniel didn't say anything after that and just ate the breakfast she served him. He wanted to stay there all day and talk to her but he had things to do. As Daniel went back outside the phone rang. Charity picked up the portable.

"Paradise Ranch. How can I help you?"

A woman responds. "Yes, I would like to make a reservation and we want to bring our grandson along, would that be a good idea? Do you have activities for a five-year-old?"

"Yes we do!" Charity replied.

"Perfect! Do you have an opening the middle of August? Josiah will be starting kindergarten this year and has been begging us all summer to learn how to ride, just like his daddy! My name is Vicki Childs by the way."

"Okay, Mrs. Childs. We will be looking for you on the fifteenth of August," Charity replied. "That is the last group we will be taking this summer. I hope you have an enjoyable time here. Have you been here before?"

"No," answered Mrs. Childs. "We haven't but we have heard a lot about it from Daniel when he comes to visit."

She about dropped the phone. "Daniel?" she squeaked.

"Yes. Daniel," replied Vicki. "He comes here for his vacation but this time Josiah wants to go see where his daddy works."

Charity was shocked by the sudden revelation but managed not to show it. "Thank you, Mrs. Childs. See you in August," she said and hung up. Thankfully she was sitting at that point because she needed to after hearing that.

Daniel…her Daniel had a son? Where was his wife? Why did she not know about this? Is this the reason Daniel was so sad? Charity was poleaxed. Daniel has a five-year-old, she couldn't believe it.

Why am I even calling him my Daniel, she wondered.

After finishing the accounts, Charity felt like she needed to talk to Jess. Walking out to the barn, Charity saw Daniel working with the newly acquired horses. As a working dude ranch, they needed horses to match every type of rider from the beginner to the experienced. This new group will be a good addition to the herd but they needed to be broken, which was why Daniel was working with them. She found Jess in the back stall with the new filly, Star. Charity had fallen in love with Star the moment she was born. Sarah had produced a beautiful cream-colored filly with a perfect white star on her forehead; her cream coloring came from her sire though, a beautiful golden palomino named Stuart.

Jess looked up as Charity walked in. "I'll be right with you!" *Something is not right,* he thought. *I could feel it in my bones.*

With Charity however, he knew he had to wait until she brought things up. After giving love to both her girls, Charity looked over at Jess.

"So what do we know about Daniel?"

Jess stood up. "What is this all about, Charity?" he asked. "The man has worked here for over three years and you are just now asking questions? What is really going on here?"

Charity explained about the phone call, and Jess stood there stroking his beard thinking.

"So Daniel has a kid. That's news to me!" Jess said, and he was surprised too. "I hired him while you were in the hospital. I didn't think to ask him those kinds of questions."

"What kind of questions did you ask then?"

"The usual, where you been working, what are your qualifications?" Jess replied. "I didn't think it mattered what his personal life was before coming here. So that's where he goes every vacation then. Hmm…good to know the man takes his responsibilities to heart."

Charity grunted and walked away muttering about men, babies, and families.

Jess just smiled and patted Sarah he said "Maybe something good will come of this old girl. This is just what Charity needs to get back on track with her life. God sure works in mysterious ways, Sarah."

She nickered and nodded her head as if she agreed.

That evening Daniel's cell rang, looking at the screen he clicked on it and answered.

"Hello, Vicki."

"Hello yourself," she replied. "We have some big news. We made reservations at your dude ranch. Josiah has been begging us all summer to go see where you work, so Josh and I decided there wasn't a better time than now since he starts kindergarten in September."

Daniel didn't know what to say. He had no right to tell them what do or where to go but he wasn't sure if he was ready to let everyone know about his past.

Oh well, I guess I must, he thought.

The next morning Charity had to go to town and get the shopping done for next week's group of clients. She called the barn to ask Jess to bring the truck to the front of the house while she finished getting ready, but Daniel answered instead.

"Jess just took Brody out for a run so I'll bring it right down," he said.

As he drove up to the front of the house, she wondered if she should mention the reservation but decided not to just yet. *Besides what could I really say*, she thought. *You didn't tell me you had a wife and kid.*

No. It was none of her business so she just smiled. "Thanks. I'll be back this afternoon. Let Jess know where I've gone when he gets back okay?"

When she got into town, she decided she might as well treat herself to a nice cold iced tea before shopping. As she walked into the diner, she saw Sophia and stopped to say hello.

"It's good to see you, Charity," Sophia said. "I'm sorry I haven't been out in the past couple of months, but Scott's parents came to live with us after his dad's stroke and between getting then settled in and work and the new baby coming, I've been pretty busy."

The statement about the new baby went right over Charity's head. "Where is that precious little boy?"

"Matthew's at home with his grandparents. I took a break and came to return the library books, want to join me? I just ordered an iced tea."

"Perfect!" Charity said. "That's what I stopped in for too!" She sat beside Sophia and called out to Amy. "Hey, Amy! Can you add another iced tea for us please?"

"Glad to. Be right with you, Charity!" Amy yelled from the counter.

They continued chatting. "How old is Matthew now, Sophia?"

Sophia smiled. "Two. You should have heard him last night at dinner, we were eating and out pops, 'Momma, if Daddy is Grandpa Steve's son, then whose son are you?' I almost had to call Doc Jensen to come over because both Scott and Steve choked on their mouthful of food. Mary and I had the hardest time not laughing aloud." They both laughed at that as Amy swung by their table to drop off their ice tea's , "Ladies I'll be right back with you" as she leaned in to serve the food to the table behind them. Charity scooted over so that Amy could grab a moment to sit. Amy winked at Charity as Sophia continued with the tale.

"Scott had to explain that mommy was not a son. 'She is a girl so she would be a daughter not a son.' Then Matthew asked, 'why don't we have a daughter?' Scott laughed at that, then he told him we will have one soon. 'Mommy has a baby in her tummy but we don't know what God has given us yet.' Scott was patting my tummy as he told them so then Matthew came back with 'Well then, can God tell me so that can I know?' I picked him up then and said, 'Okay young man enough of the questions. It's time for you to get in your pajamas and go to bed.' And he said, 'Aw Mom, do I have to?' And I told him, 'yes, you have to! But first you must kiss daddy goodnight and I will read you one story tonight." Amy

reached across Charity and grabbed Sophia's hand, "Oh congratulations Sophia, you and Scott must be so happy."
"Well ladies, it's time for this young lady to get back to work." Amy hops out of the booth and disappears into the kitchen.

Charity gushed as she turned to hug her. "You're pregnant? Congratulations! How far along are you?"

"Five months," said Sophia. "And Scott told me last night that this was to be my last month to work. Mary is busy with caring for Steve full-time, so I can see his point. Besides, I think I'm ready to be a full-time mom. How about you, are you seeing anyone? You love kids and would make a great mom."

Charity squirmed and looked down at her injured leg. "I don't think I ever will be."

Sophia smiled. "Just you wait. When the right man comes along, he won't even notice your leg, and you'll know when he comes along!"

However Charity already did want to but was scared to open up her heart to hurt because all that ever happens is, you love someone, then something happens and you are left hurting. *No thank you*, she said to herself. *I don't want to hurt anymore!* Another emotion inside her was saying to forgive.

When she entered the store after sharing an afternoon tea with Sophia, she saw Pastor Mark and made sure to go in the opposite direction but he was determined to speak with her.

"Good morning, Charity. How's the leg doing? I see you are limping less—the physical therapy seems to have done its job," Pastor Mark said when he caught up to her. "My wife Nancy said she was impressed with your determination to conquer walking. We sure miss seeing you at church and hearing your golden voice. Things just haven't been the same in the choir."

"Thank you but I'm just not up to attending yet," Charity mumbled.

Pastor Mark sighed. "Well when you are ready, we will be there with outstretched arms."

Charity quickly walked away and wondered why she even cared that Pastor Mark looked somewhat disappointed with her answer. She was almost through at the checkout stand when she saw Nathaniel's grandmother, Mrs. Davis, enter the store.

Maybe she won't see me, hoped Charity.

Nonetheless, just like it had been with Pastor Mark, Mrs. Davis seemed determined and she called out to her.

"Charity, it's so good to see you here. I've been praying for you." She continued talking as she walked over to the checkout stand. "Are you going to attend the church's Fourth of July picnic this year? We missed you last year, I'm in charge of the pie booth this year, and I am supposed to call people to donate. You were next on my list. Can I put you down for a few? I've tried but I just can't get my crusts to turn out as you and your mom's always were."

Charity swallowed. "Um sure. How many would you like?"

Mrs. Davis smiled sweetly. "How many can I ask you for?"

Charity couldn't help it, she burst out laughing. "Mrs. Davis you are something else! How many were you thinking of asking me for?"

She smiled again "Would ten be too many to ask for?"

"Ten?" Cindy, the cashier burst out laughing too. "Wow, Charity! Ten pies? Seems like she is hoping you would make most of them for her. Last year they only got ten pies out of people."

Mrs. Davis giggled. "Cindy, you hit the nail on the head. Nobody comes close to making pies like Charity and her mother did. I've asked quite a few people but so far I only had two willing to commit."

Charity went still for a moment and both Mrs. Davis and Cindy were silent.

She finally looked up. "Why not? Okay, yes I'll make you ten pies, any kind in particular you want?"

All smiles now Mrs. Davis said, "Well…"

And once again Charity and Cindy both burst out laughing.

"Watch out Charity, the next thing you know she will be saying I want ten different kinds," Cindy said.

"Okay Mrs. Davis, I will on one condition!"

"What's that, Charity?"

"I get to be the one to decide what kind and how many kinds, okay?"

Smiling that sweet grandmotherly smile of hers she replied, "That's fair, but I want ten big pies not the minis like you made for the mother-daughter tea that one year!"

"I remember that, they were so cute!" Cindy said. "That was the last year that my mom was able to attend before Dad got so sick." Cindy looked away then. Charity knew just how she felt.

"So Cindy has your mom and Doc Jensen returned from their honeymoon yet?"

Cindy looked up with a smile. "Yes they got home last week! Mom looks so happy, Doc has made her smile and laugh again, and it's so good to see her that way again."

There were silent for a moment, then Cindy spoke up.

"Hey, Charity. Is Daniel still working for you? How can you get anything done with a hunk like that around? Can a guy look any better in clothes? Have you ever seen a brighter sky than those eyes of his?"

Charity started blushing. "Oh does he have blue eyes, Cindy? I hadn't noticed."

Mrs. Davis looked at the two and just smiled. *So that's the way it is*, she thought. *Charity is in love! It's about time.*

"Charity Stewart, are you going to just stand there and tell me you haven't noticed him? What is wrong with you?" Cindy yelled.

Charity put her hand on Cindy's "Whoa calm down now, Cindy. Okay, yes I have noticed! But what do you want me to do about it?"

"I know what I would do about it."

"Oh and what is that?" Charity asked.

"I would tell him," Cindy's quickly replied.

"Really, Cindy? You would walk right up to him and say you have the prettiest blue eyes and you look great in those painted on jeans and shirt?"

Cindy smiled. "Well not exactly like that. Hey wait a minute I didn't mention him looking like his clothes were painted on."

Charity blushed again. "Oops, look at that, your line is starting to back up, I got to go." She grabbed her bags and fled the store. Mrs. Davis and Cindy just looked at each other and they both knew something was brewing.

On the ride home, Charity kept muttering about sassy cashiers, nosy grandmas, and thinking about Daniel's blue, blue eyes.

I am in big trouble, she thought.

As she pulled up to the house, Jess was sitting on the porch swing waiting for her.

"Hey I got a call from a Mrs. Childs just now she wants to know if Daniel will be working when they come or if he'll be able to take his vacation then."

She barked out as she stomped into the house still feeling a bit testy, "Ask him yourself"

Jess just grinned and yelled back, "Maybe I will!"

Muttering as she was putting away the groceries, Charity was in no mood for Daniel when he walked in just then.

She turned to him. "And just what do you want, mister?" she shouted.

CHAPTER 8

Daniel just stared at her, surprised by her sudden crankiness. "Maybe I should come back later and speak with you when you're in a better mood."

Charity sighed. "Never mind. I'm sorry I snapped at you, it's been a rough morning so far."

Daniel grinned. "Does it have anything to do with something about ten pies?"

Charity grinned then too and remarked, "You've heard about that already?"

"Yup. Mrs. Davis called and told me to ask you if you would consider making at least one chocolate cream pie."

"She did? I told her I would make the pies on one condition, that I get to choose the kind and how many of each."

Daniel just grinned again. "Okay I confess she didn't ask me that. She told me the condition but I thought it wouldn't hurt to ask because that is my favorite."

Charity swatted him playfully on the arm. "Oh really? Good to know. But I have to get dinner started so get out of my kitchen!"

"Okay but we both know that really isn't what I came in to say, I just thought I could get a pie for myself out of this."

He grinned and grabbed an apple as he went out the door. Charity just shook her head and smiled. *Now I need to make a chocolate pie for tonight's dessert.*

Daniel went back out to the corral and shared his apple with Brody.

"Charity would want you to have some too," he said to the horse.

He knew it was time to talk with Jess about Josiah and the Childs. After Daniel finished telling Jess everything he felt better, another portion of his pain disappeared. Just by acknowledging to others about his son made him feel better. Time really does heal all wounds; his was now disappearing, especially after spending some time with Charity. He grinned as he thought of her.

Jess came up to the house before dinner. "Charity, I told Daniel he could take his vacation time while his in-laws and son are here, I hope you don't mind?"

"Why would I, Jess? You're in charge."

Jess laughed. "Am I hearing you right? Yum, something sure smells good! What's for dinner?"

"Chicken pot pie and we have chocolate cream pie for dessert!" Charity answered. "I seem to have pie on my mind after my run in with Mrs. Davis this morning."

"I don't mind, I get to reap the benefits of it."

Charity just laughed. "Just go ring the supper bell please, it's time to eat!"

The men then came in, and Charity brought the food to the table. Jess said the grace and they all dug in. As they ate, Charity reminded everyone the next group of clients would be arriving in three days.

"Is everything all set up and ready?" she asked the men.

"I got the guest cabins all cleaned and stocked up," Toby replied, "So have we heard from Simon as to when he will return?"

"Yes, he called yesterday and said they had just come back from the doctors and his brothers cast finally came off, he said it's about time too, because he misses Sarah and wants to see that filly of hers."

Toby said, "Okay then I'll make sure his room will be ready then too."

"Thanks, Toby. You really stepped up and filled in for Simon while he was gone." She then addressed all of them. "Boys?" she asked.

"Are you going to miss Toby's cooking?"

"Uh sure thing, Miss Charity," they all sputtered and choked then hid their grins behind their napkins.

"Hey, no fair guys no one else wanted to do it. I can't help it that the only thing I can make is beans and corn bread! Good thing we didn't have clients here, they would have left for sure!" Toby said.

They all laughed.

Charity interrupted the laughter. "I doubt I could compete with your cooking skills, Toby." Nevertheless, she couldn't help it and she laughed aloud herself.

"Miss Charity, not even cook can compete against you. You're the best and a whole lot prettier too!" Toby declared.

"Well thank you again, Toby. And on that note, who's ready for dessert?"

They all spoke up. "We are!"

"I saw it as I went out to ring the bell and it sure looked mighty yummy," Jess said. "We're having chocolate cream pie."

As he said that Daniel looked directly into Charity's eyes and smiled. "Sounds good to me because that's my favorite."

Jess took note of that and the blush that was staining Charity's cheeks.

The next day Simon arrived home and settled back in. Jess filled him in on how many to expect in the next group and what had gone on while he was gone. He was glad Simon was back, he sure had missed his checkers partner. He even told Simon what he had seen developing between Daniel and Charity.

"Anything I can do to help it along?" Simon asked.

"Don't know but guess what? Mrs. Davis cornered her at the grocery store and roped her into making ten pies for the church's annual Fourth of July picnic."

Simon chuckled. "Good. It's way past time for Charity to get back to church."

Then Jess and Simon settled down to the job of playing checkers.

Ah, Jess thought. *It sure is good to have my old friend back.*

━╱╲━

The phone kept ringing and no one seemed to be answering it, so Daniel ran in from the corral and grabbed it.

"Paradise Ranch, how can I help you?"

A familiar voice responded to him. "Is this Jess? This is Virginia Davis, I heard Simon came home. How is his brother now?"

"Ah, Mrs. Davis this isn't Jess. It's Daniel. Hold on and let me get Jess for you, or do you really want Simon?"

"Oh, no thank you young man that won't be necessary. I'll talk to Jess."

Daniel smiled. "Okay Mrs. Davis, hold on. Oh by the way, thank you for calling yesterday! I got a chocolate pie out of it."

"Come again, what was that?" Virginia sputtered.

"After you called yesterday, I decided to see if I could influence Charity's choice of pies by saying you had requested one, when she huffed that her one condition was that she got to pick, I confessed that it was all me and that it was my favorite."

Mrs. Davis laughed. "Well good for you, that girl needs someone like you to get her back on track."

"Hold on now, Mrs. Davis, I just had a hankering for chocolate pie. Here comes Jess now Mrs. Davis." He then handed the phone off to Jess. "It's Mrs. Davis."

Daniel returned to the stable. The horses were so much easier to deal with, and he still had to get this latest group of horses ready for the ranch work and in just a little over a month. Josiah was coming, he sure was looking forward to that.

Charity had decided she didn't need to book any more groups after the one with Daniel's in-laws and son. *I get the ranch back to myself*, she thought.

She was grateful it had become a working dude ranch since that was what had saved the ranch while she was in the hospital, but so many changes.

Why God, why did you take them all from me? Especially since it was, just two days after Jimmy had dumped me for Lucy. There I was , thinking he was going to propose and instead he tells me he had fallen in love with Lucy.

Charity sighed and cried out. "I don't need a husband, and the ranch is doing just fine!"

Then out through the window, she saw Daniel and she knew she's lying to herself. *Why does this man affect me so much, God? Wait, why am I talking to God? I'm still mad at him.* Then it dawned on her that her pain was subsiding, especially whenever she thought of or saw Daniel. *Oh well, I need to get to work on those pies. The Fourth is coming up fast and I haven't even decided what kinds to make.*

After deciding which kinds of pie to make, Charity knew she needed to run into town to get the ingredients for them. The picnic was in two days. *Why did I let her talk me into making these pies? I can do this, just make the pies, drop them off and get out of there. I can do this,* she kept repeating to herself.

Once she got to the grocery store, she went to the baking aisle and got her sugar and flour then over to the produce where she grabbed her fruit and impulsively she went back to the baking aisle.

I might as well make a chocolate cream pie too, she thought.

When she had everything she needed she headed to the checkout lane, Cindy was working.

"Oh today must be the day," she remarked as Charity rang her up. "Can I come to your house and watch and maybe sample as you are baking?"

Charity smiled. "Sounds good! I'd love some company, but don't you think that your boss would be kind of upset that you left work?"

"Probably, but then my body is saying 'give me sweets!'"

They both laughed and said good-bye. Just as Charity was walking out the door, Pastor Mark's wife Nancy walked in and she stopped to say hello.

"Charity I heard you were making some pies for this year's Fourth of July Picnic."

"Yes, Mrs. Davis asked me for ten."

"Ten?" Nancy laughed. "Is that all? I am so glad that I can't bake all that well. Ten pies…oh my! Well I won't keep you, it looks as if today is the day you intend to make them, and so I shall see you at the picnic." Then she continued walking into the store as Charity walked out of the store.

When she got back home, she began making her pies, baking them reminded her of her mother and all the times they used to do this together. She had to take a deep breath. "I think mom would approve!" Then she realized that a little more of her anger was disappearing.

The morning of the fourth, Charity got up and started making breakfast. She had told Jess the night before to tell the men breakfast would be at eight. By then, all the morning chores would be done, after that they would have the rest of the day off to attend the picnic, that was just another of her parent's traditions.

This morning she was making fresh blueberry muffins, hash browns, and ham and cheese omelets. As the muffins were ready to come out of the oven, she heard the door open. It was the men. *Perfect, right on time*, she thought.

She put them in a basket and brought everything to the table. The men were waiting for her before sitting down. Jess asked Simon to say Grace, and he happily obliged.

"Lord, we thank you for Miss Charity and for her good food, bless this day and bless the picnic and keep safe all the families that are coming, Amen."

Charity looked up. "Thank you, Simon. Now men let's sit and eat!"

After everyone had eaten, they all picked up their dishes and headed to the kitchen, then out the door to get ready to head to town. Jess and Daniel hung around. Jess grabbed the sponge and went out to clean the table as Daniel started filling up the sink with soap and hot water, then Jess came back in grabbed a towel to start drying the dishes.

Charity looked at them both. "What are you two doing? Get out of here and go get ready, I will finish this up and will be ready to go in an hour."

"No," they said at the same time. Then Daniel said for both of them,

"You go get ready, you've already done enough this morning, we will do this, then we will pack up the pies," Daniel said.

Charity shook her head. "Okay if you insist, you won't get an argument out of me!" Then she walked out. *Might as well do as I am told*, she thought.

She went upstairs and took extra care when getting ready. As she came down the stairs, Daniel was waiting for her in the kitchen.

"Where's Jess?" she asked.

"Oh he and Simon just left with all the pies and asked me to drive you into town," Daniel replied.

Charity gulped. "Um I was going to drive myself."

Daniel grinned. "Then Jess was right, you were just going to drop the pies off and then leave, weren't you?"

Charity knew when she was beat so she sighed. "Okay then I guess I'm ready, let's go and get this thing over with."

Daniel looked at her and grinned closed her door and walked around to the driver's side once in the truck Daniel looked over at her. "May I ask you a question?"

"That all depends on the question," Charity quipped as she kept her eyes focused on the familiar landscape of the road into town to avoid looking directly in his eyes.

He laughed. "Cautious are you?"

Charity grinned. "Yes, I am! Now what did you want to ask?" They were coming up to the bridge where her life had changed in a moment, Charity took a deep breath and at the last moment turned to look Daniel directly in the eye instead of looking at it. Although it looked nothing like it did that night Charity still had a hard time looking at. Daniel's smile disappeared. "Why have you isolated yourself since you came home from the hospital? Jess said before the accident you were the most active girl in town, you knew everyone and knew no strangers."

Charity looked over at him. "Because my life ended the day I came out of the coma and was told my family had died!"

That statement caught Daniel's attention so he dragged his gaze back to her from the rolling hills he had come to love so much.

"No it didn't, Charity. Look around you, you have your health, the Ranch, the men here who depend on you, the community came to cheer you up for a while but you kept turning them away. They care about you or they wouldn't have come, even now Mrs. Davis said she asked you to make pies just so that you would get involved again!"

"People should just leave me alone," Charity muttered.

"No," Daniel said. "They shouldn't. They love you, why can't you accept that love?"

Charity turned to face him "Because I'm not worth it. God took my family and the man I thought I loved all within a few days of each other."

Daniel hit the brakes. "What did you just say?"

With tears running down her face she replied, "I'm not worth loving. Just ask Jimmy. Two days before the accident he asked me to meet him in our special place, and I thought this is it. He's going to ask me to marry him and do you know what he said?" She didn't wait for Daniel's response. "He said, 'I'm sorry Charity, I'm in love with Lucy and we are leaving town the day after Stephen's party to get married.' I congratulated them and just walked away, two days later the accident happened. God doesn't love me anymore."

Daniel had already pulled the truck over to the side of the road. He reached out and pulled Charity over to his side and just let her cry.

"That's not true Charity, God does love you." *Moreover,* he thought, *so do I.*

But he wasn't ready to tell her that just yet, she wasn't ready to hear it and he wasn't sure if he was either. However, seeing her crying made him realize that he was ready to love and that she was the one. God had sent him here to find her. Now he just had to get her to realize the same thing.

After Charity's tears had dried up she said, "I must look a mess."

To that remark, Daniel replied, "Not to me."

She half smiled. "Okay we can go now I'm through crying," she said, wiping her face. "Thanks. I don't know what just came over me to blurt that out. I've only told Amy about what Jimmy did. It was when she came to ask me to be her maid of honor. She promised not to say anything about it though to anyone until I was ready."

"Then no one ever questioned me about it after I got out of the hospital, Jess told me that he had just up and moved out of town the day after the accident and no one had heard from him since."

"Good thing too," Daniel said and started the truck up again.

When they finally arrived, Jess looked at them and Daniel gave him a look that said *not now, I'll explain later*. He proceeded to keep Charity busy the rest of the day and made sure to keep her by his side. When the fireworks started that evening, Daniel had seen to it that Charity had gone around to everyone there and at least said hello. Everyone had said they were glad that she made it this year, how they had enjoyed her pies and commented on how well she was doing and asking when would she be up to attending church again and get back in the choir. Daniel took note of all those things and decided right then that he would talk to Jess about her life before the accident.

It had been decided before the fireworks were to start that some of the ranch hands would go home in time to do the evening chores and return as usual they were all going to sit together to watch the fireworks. Some things just never seemed to change.

Daniel had arranged that he would be the one to drive Charity home, he wanted to talk to her about everyone's comments but Jess walked up to them.

"Can I hitch a ride with you two?"

"Sounds good to me," Charity and Daniel simultaneously answered. They both laughed.

Jess just grinned, thinking there sure seems to be something going on here. When the fireworks were over, they gathered up all their belongings and headed back to the parking lot. On their way though, Mrs. Davis had stopped Jess to ask him something. As they waited for Jess to catch up, Daniel seemed as though he wanted to say something but right then Jess arrived.

"Charity will you sit in the middle, I'm getting to old to straddle the gear shift and still be comfortable," Jess requested as he opened the car door.

Daniel thought that was a great idea, this way Charity would still be by his side.

When they arrived at the ranch, Jess waited until Charity had opened the door and gone inside.

"Okay Daniel out with it," Jess commanded. "What happened on the way to the picnic? why were you two late?"

He proceeded to tell Jess what Charity had told him about Jimmy.

"I never knew. Oh my poor girl!" Jess exclaimed. "If I ever see that man again I'm going to give him a piece of my mind." He huffed off and went to his room.

CHAPTER 9

They next day as she was finishing her laundry, the door-bell rang. She went to answer it and opened the door to find Mrs. Davis, Pastor Mark, and Doc Jensen.

"To what do I owe the pleasure of all three of you coming today?" Charity smirked.

"We just had to thank you in person for the pies you contributed," Pastor Mark responded.

Charity made a face. "Yeah right, you might as well come in and tell me what you really want?"

"Well…" he paused. "It's about your pies."

She wasn't able to hide her concern. "Why? What was wrong with them, did someone get sick?"

It was Doc who answered her. "No, why would you think that?"

"Because I didn't think you had anything to do with the picnic or the pie booth," Charity said.

"I don't but my wife does," he replied. "But today she and Cindy are spending the day together, saying something about working on the honeymoon album."

By then they had all come in and Charity had served them coffee and iced tea. Pastor Mark waited until Charity sat down before speaking up.

"Since your pies sold before anyone else's and all through the day people were commenting on them, I thought I should approach you in person. You know we have a prison ministry at the church and this year we wanted to do something special for the Bible study participants for the fourth. We were told by the warden that we couldn't do it on the fourth but we could do it on the next scheduled Bible Study, which is next Friday."

"We were thinking of having a pie and ice cream social for them," Mrs. Davis piped up.

Charity gulped. "Stop right there, Mrs. Davis. I know you are Nathaniel's grandmother but I don't really want anything to do with him just yet," she croaked, the smile on her face gone. "I understand that he has done well there and is even taking courses to become a pastor so he can lead the Bible study, but I'm sorry I haven't forgiven him or God yet completely for the accident. Maybe later I'll be ready but not at this time."

Mrs. Davis reached out and placed her hand on Charity's, "I know, honey and that is exactly why I asked Pastor Mark and Doc to come with me. Can we pray with you right now and let you think about it for a day or so?"

"Yes but don't expect any miracles," Charity said. "The pain and anger is just beginning to fade a little but it's still there."

They all gathered in a circle and joined hands, Pastor Mark started and they went around the circle, when it came time for Charity's turn she politely declined and then Pastor Mark closed the prayer.

"Charity I want you to really pray about this tonight," Doc almost begged. "I, more than the others, know what it cost you just to stay in the room right now. Thank you for agreeing to hear us out. I do know that your body can't heal completely until the body and the mind are in complete alignment. But just look at you, yesterday you actually looked and acted like the old Charity. It's my opinion that this just may be the catalyst that sparks that alignment."

They all stood then and bid goodbye. "We'll be praying for you and be sure to pray yourself. We love you and only want the best for you," Mrs. Davis said before heading for the door.

After they left, Charity sat down to think about what they had said, but she realized that they really didn't get to *say* anything other than introduce the concept because she had closed the door on that conversation immediately.

I wonder what it is they really wanted of me, she thought.

Looking at the clock on the mantel, she decided they would've had the time to get back to town and get to their respective homes. *I'll just call Pastor Mark and ask him.* She dialed his number but Nancy answered.

"No, Charity he isn't here. But he should be in his office at the church. Can I take a message for him or will you call him there?"

"No need to leave a message. I'll call the church and talk to him," she said and hung up.

Just then, the phone rang. It was Mrs. Davis.

"I hope I'm not interrupting anything but as we were driving back to town we all realized that we hadn't even told you what we actually wanted you to do. This way you can pray more specifically then just generally," she said. "What we were thinking was seeing if you would be willing to come to the jail and bring your guitar to lead the praise music and contribute some pies of course! Pastor Mark said his wife will bring her ice cream maker and Mrs. Jensen will bring hers and I'm bringing mine. Hold on a minute Pastor Mark is making interrupting motions with his hand in my face. Stop that Pastor Mark what is it that I have forgotten?" Charity hears mummering in the background, then Mrs. Davis gets back on the line, "Pastor Mark just wanted to reminded me to let you know there are only 30 that signed up for the Bible study, but that is only because that's all the warden would allow for a non-prison gathering. So I was thinking with three ice cream makers, we can offer different flavors! Therefore, we were wondering if you had a ranch hand that could come and help with the cranking, say that nice young man Daniel. In addition, would you mind if I asked for eight pies? That way the men can each have large slices of the pie and we still would have enough to serve the helpers and the warden."

"Okay," Charity responded. "Now that I know what it is you need of me, I can pray about providing it. Are you sure you haven't forgotten anything else Mrs. Davis? Like would you really be requiring me to attend?" Charity asked in the hopes that she wouldn't have to make an appearance.

"That's up to you, if you just want to provide the pies and a ranch hand we will understand," the old lady paused. "Although we would love for you to be there to lead the praise music too."

"Okay, Mrs. Davis. Thanks for letting me know." (Who would have thought that sweet little Mrs. Davis would be a talker?)

That night Charity did pray about it halfheartedly, although she didn't understand why she was praying in the first place.

In the morning, Charity headed over to the bunkhouse looking for Jess, she needed to talk to Jess about whom he would recommend for the job. She decided she would make the pies and supply a ranch hand but that was it. That isn't what her heart was telling her though, because she loved music and enjoyed playing her guitar. She was just avoiding the visit to prison because she didn't want to see Nathaniel.

"Nope, not going to do it," Jess declared.

"Why not?" Charity said.

Jess fired back immediately. "If you don't volunteer to go, then no one from this ranch will go."

Charity was both shocked and puzzled. Since she didn't respond, Jess continued with his rant. "It's way past time to for you to forgive him. He needs that forgiveness from you, Charity."

"You're right, okay I concede," Charity muttered. "I'll call Mrs. Davis and let her know. Now who will you volunteer from the hands?"

"Daniel," he told her.

"Jess stop trying to be a matchmaker, he isn't interested in me."

Jess smiled. "I do believe you are wrong, young lady, but that is who I choose."

"Fine, have it your way. I'll call her from the house though." She stomped off. Simon chuckled from behind Jess.

"Good for you, Jess," Simon remarked. "Next time though, don't be so obvious. She'll learn at her own pace."

As Charity came through the kitchen door, she was still muttering to herself about nosy old matchmaking men. Then she thought about it and giggled. *I guess I do need a good dressing down every now and then*, she said to herself.

She decided to phone Mrs. Davis about the change of plans. When the old lady's phone rang a few minutes later, she knew it would be Charity.

"Hello, Charity?" she answered.

"Hello Mrs. Davis," Charity said. "I'm calling you back to let you know that I'll do the praise music and supply the pies and the ranch hand to help out."

"Oh thank you Charity," Mrs. Davis happily said. "I'll let the others on the committee know, and I won't ask for any special kinds of pie either."

CHAPTER 10

Friday arrived faster than Charity had thought possible. All the pies are ready. She just had to gather up her courage to actually go. Precisely at four-thirty in the afternoon, Daniel knocked on the door.

"Everything all ready to go?" he asked.

"All but me," Charity responded.

Daniel looked at her. "Are you sure you want to do this?"

"No, I'm not sure. But Jess kind of goaded me into accepting."

"Okay. Then let's pack everything in the truck and get going."

Daniel was silent as they drove to the prison. Charity on the other hand was uncomfortable with the silence, and so she finally started some conversation.

"I know I need to forgive him. But he did take my family away from me."

Daniel looked her way and replied, "Sometimes we need forgiveness before we can forgive ourselves."

Charity noted that he had that sadness in his eyes again. She wanted to ask him about it but she wasn't sure if she wanted to get that intimate with him while struggling with the same feelings right now, so she let the remark pass, for the time being at least.

They had arrived Charity could see Pastor Mark and the others standing by the church van waiting for them. Charity was chanting quietly. "Okay I can do this."

Daniel looked her way. "What did you say?"

Charity turned away from the man who seemed to notice all her moods and answered him. "I was just chanting I could do this."

He gave her a look saying he understood. They got out of his truck and walked over to the others.

"Do we have to be searched?" Charity asked.

They all shook their heads. As they entered in the gates, Charity had a moment of panic. *What am I doing here?* She then took a deep breath and felt better.

She saw him as soon as they walked into the room. He saw her at the same moment and started to walk over to her. Unknowingly, she stepped a little closer to Daniel. He looked down at her and whispered.

"It will be okay, Charity."

As Nathaniel got closer, she noticed some differences in him since the last time she had seen him. There was a glow radiating from him, but there was sadness there also. He looked her in the eye.

"Charity, I know I don't deserve it but could you please find it in your heart to forgive me?" Nathaniel begged, almost in tears. "These past three years, I've had a lot of time to reflect on what I did that day and how it affected so many people. I want you to know that if I could I would change back time and not do what I had done."

Tears were streaming down her face as he spoke. Daniel reached out his hand and she gripped it so fiercely, but he knew he wouldn't say a word about it. This was what she needed right now. Charity tried to speak but nothing came out so she cleared her throat and tried again. The second time her voice came out strong.

"Nathaniel, thank you," she mumbled. "I know you mean what you say, I can see it in your face and yes it is time I give you my forgiveness." As she spoke those words, her heart lightened a little more.

"May I hug you?" Nathaniel asked.

"Of course, that's what you do when you forgive someone."

Then they proceeded with the social and the evening ended with Nathaniel giving a Bible study on overcoming the enemy.

When he was through Charity walked over to him and told him that was the best Bible study she had attended in years. Pastor Mark overhead that remark and smiled. Truth is, it was the only Bible study she had been to in over three years.

On the way home Charity glanced at Daniel, the sadness was there again. *What caused the sadness,* she wondered.

Daniel glanced over to Charity when she wasn't looking and thought, *I wonder if this is the right time to talk about Josiah and his mother. If she forgave Nathaniel for what he did, maybe she can offer me forgiveness too. It was too late to ask Victoria for hers.*

He thought about it a few more minutes and decided to tell her, just at the same moment she had decided to ask him about his sadness.

"I was wondering…" they said at the same time. They looked at each other's eyes for a moment, not talking.

It was Charity who broke it off. "You go first."

Daniel took a couple of deep breaths. "No, ladies first."

"Coward," she automatically responded, as if it was her brother next to her. She felt drawn to him but somehow not in a brotherly manner. "Okay here goes…" She heaved a sigh and went on. "I see sadness in your eyes, and I want to know why and how I can help you fix it."

He looked shocked. "I didn't think anyone could see."

"Daniel, why are you so sad?"

He looked at her and asked, "Can this wait until we stop driving, it's big, for me at least."

Charity nodded.

CHAPTER 11

Once they had pulled up the driveway, Charity invited him into the house.

"Come in, and I'll put on a pot of coffee if you want."

"If you don't mind," he replied.

She went about making the coffee and got out two cups. When it was done she sat down across him.

"Okay, out with it," Charity ordered.

Daniel breathed deeply and began his confession. "You already know about my having a son but you don't know the rest. I didn't love Victoria. It was our first date, and she wanted to go to this party. I didn't really want to go but we did anyway. When we got there, everyone was drinking and they offered us some. She grabbed one quickly, so I decided to have one too. I don't drink by the way. Well—" he drank some coffee—"the alcohol went right to me. Victoria was hanging all over me and wanted to go upstairs. I guess I let her take me up there and we... we apparently did it. I don't remember, actually. Then

I didn't see her until two months later when she came knocking at my door looking for me. She told me she was pregnant. Naturally, I asked if she was sure. She told me 'of course I'm sure.' To this day, I still don't remember having done anything with her that night. The next day we went to the courthouse took the blood test and ten days after that we were married. I was so ashamed of what I had done.

May I have a refill please? He hands her the cup, as he released the cup into her hands he felt something like an electrical jolt. He quickly pulled away wondering if only he felt it or if she did too, her expression didn't give any indication as she took the cup and turned to refill it. He did note though that Charity made sure that there was no contact between them when she put his cup down (in front of him). Daniel decided to act as if nothing had happened, he waited until she sat back down before continuing on with his confession.

"When she went into labor I was away on a job, but her parents called and told me about it afterwards. I rushed back to town and went to see him," he paused and smiled in nostalgia. "He was so beautiful, and I fell in love with him immediately. Since I was working out of town I left him with her parents. They wanted to raise him. Josiah doesn't look like me much, but I love him no matter what. I had once thought about getting a DNA test done, but it wouldn't really matter to me. But I never had the opportunity to ask for her forgiveness. I should have been there for her, I should have loved her." He buried his face on his hands.

Charity quickly got out of her chair and knelt before him. "Daniel, do you really think that she would have lied to you about being the father? And that she wouldn't have given you her forgiveness if you had been there? No matter what, he's still your son—you love him and provided for him. Now that he is older you could start thinking about you two being together all the time."

He looked up. "I could bring him here and live with me?"

"Oh, Daniel. If that's what you really want then yes, of course you can bring him here."

He needed time to think this through some more. "I'm tired right now, so I'll take my leave. See you in the morning." He almost leaned in to give her a hug but he refrained and walked out the door instead.

"Yes, see you in the morning."

That night Charity prayed for both Daniel and Josiah. She realized it was truly time for her to go back to church.

On Saturday night, she pulled Daniel aside.

"Would you like to go with me to church in the morning?"

"Yes, I would"

Jess was nearby and heard it all. He sent up a silent prayer of thanks as he went out to the bunkhouse and told Simon what he had just overheard. On Sunday morning during breakfast, she announced that she would be going to church with them.

When they arrived at the church, Pastor Mark was standing at the door smiling and welcoming everyone. He smiled as he spied Charity and Daniel together. Simon and Jess had called him last night and told him that God was working in both their lives to heal them.

Charity was hesitant about sitting in the front pew, but Daniel just grabbed her hand and pulled her to it, next to all the ranch hands. Nevertheless, it felt right to be sitting next to Daniel in this pew.

Daniel leaned over to her and remarked, "I can't wait until the singing starts. I didn't know until the Bible study how beautiful your voice was."

Charity bowed her head for the opening prayer and whispered, "Thank You." Then when the singing began, Charity noticed that Daniel's deep bass voice caused rumblings inside of her.

That has never happened before, she thought.

On Monday morning, Pastor Mark came to visit. He expressed his happiness at seeing her at church yesterday and wanted to thank her personally for helping with the prison ministry last Friday. Charity had already offered him coffee and while they were seated in the living room, she faced him and said, "Pastor Mark, I realize now that I need to thank you for ganging up on me to get back involved in life and church."

"Nathaniel's bible study on overcoming the enemy hit home. I've been wallowing in my own grief and missing out on all the wonderful people that I do still have in my life."

"No thanks are necessary, Charity. But you are welcome."

Then they talked more about the Bible study at the prison, and Charity asked if she could volunteer.

"Of course, we always need volunteers," Pastor Mark admitted. "Well, I need to be going. I have other stops to make today. I'll have someone on the committee get in touch with you."

He started to get up but decided against it. "But the real reason I came here today was the choir. I noticed yesterday that Daniel has a good voice. I was wondering if you could ask him if he would like to join. I stopped in at the stables first, but Jess said that he was out in the south pasture already."

"Of course, I'll ask him for you later today."

Pastor Mark smiled. "You will be joining us again, won't you?"

Charity grinned. "Just try and keep me away."

Charity went to the stables after the pastor left to go talk with Jess. She told him why the pastor was looking for Daniel and asked him to relay the message when he came back.

"No problem Charity," Jess promised. "I can do that. Am I wrong to assume that you will be joining them also?"

She grinned and nodded her head. Jess thought it was about time. When she left to go back to the house, he headed directly to the bunkhouse to tell Simon. Both the men were happy that Charity was finally healing and becoming more like the old Charity.

That afternoon Mrs. Davis called. She explained that the pastor had called to let her know that Charity wanted to volunteer. "We meet Tuesday afternoons at 4 p.m. See you then?" Charity affirmed it.

When Daniel got back to the stable Jess hollered from the office.

"Daniel, can you come in here for a minute. You had a visitor today."

"A visitor?" Daniel asked as he came walking in.

"Yes, a visitor. Pastor Mark stopped by, he wants to know if you would consider joining the choir."

Daniel stalled for a moment before he answered him. "The choir?"

"Yes, you know, a group of people standing up front singing."

"I know what a choir is. Why me is what I am wondering?"

"Because he heard you singing yesterday and the choir needs another bass, also an alto but Charity already told him she would be joining them again."

Daniel's eyes lit up when Jess mentioned Charity's name. "Okay then, I'll call him and get the particulars. Thanks, Jess."

That evening instead of him calling the pastor, he approached Charity about it. He couldn't help it—she just drew him to her. Charity was secretly excited about Daniel joining the choir.

I'll get the chance to be around him more, she said to herself. Charity told him practice is on Thursday nights at 7 p.m.

"We can drive in together. Do you want to call the pastor or shall I?"

"I will call him," Daniel replied.

At three on Tuesday afternoon, Charity called down to the stable to let Jess know that she was leaving to go to the prison ministry meeting. He told her to drive safely, and it felt like she had a parent. *That's a good feeling*, Charity thought.

Once she had arrived, the meeting began. Afterwards, Mrs. Davis stopped her.

"Charity, you just don't realize how much you forgiving Nathaniel means. When I spoke with my daughter-in-law, she broke down and cried. Lately she has been asking about church and wanting to come but was afraid because my son isn't too happy with her decision. He did tell her she could come if she wished, but by herself. May I introduce you to her this Sunday when I bring her?"

"Of course, but why would my forgiving him be the catalyst to her coming to church?" "Because she needed to see forgiveness in action before she was ready to commit. Thank you so much, Charity. I've been praying for her to make this step for several years, ever since Nathaniel was sentenced, that's when she started to ask all about our church." That statement humbled Charity.

On Thursday evening, Charity and Daniel headed into town for choir practice. That was the start of both of them spending a lot more time together and getting to know one another better. For Charity, that meant her heart was opening up again to life—it felt right. For Daniel, that made him yearn for Charity more, but this time he would keep his wits about him at all times and do things the right way.

Sunday morning is hectic, that much Charity remembered from when her Mom was alive. *How did she do it*, she wondered. Breakfast for fifteen and trying to get supper started before leaving for church. Not quite used to having to do that, Charity was running behind, until Simon arrived and offered to help.

While he worked on getting supper in the pan, Charity made breakfast she asked Simon how her mom had done it all.

"Think back to when your mom was alive and what she did," Simon said.

Charity thought about it and remarked, "She got things ready on Saturday night. Thank you, Simon. I'm just beginning to realize how organized mom really was."

Simon laughed. "She wasn't always, took her awhile to figure out a system, many Sunday mornings she would be late or forget about supper and then when we got home had to find something to fix that was quick and easy. After a couple of those Sundays I volunteered to help her out."

Charity looked at him. "I never knew that, thank you Simon." "Like mother like Daughter, don't worry you'll get things figured out too."

CHAPTER 12

Jess hung up the phone and then walked up to the house.

"Charity! Charity, where are you?" He heard her answer from the laundry room and went to talk with her. "I need to take a week off."

"Why, Jess?"

"My sister just called, her daughter Katrina is getting married. Seems like it's all of a sudden but nevertheless, she wants me to walk her down the aisle."

"Sure, Jess no problem. When are you leaving?"

"They booked a train ticket for me, I'll leave tomorrow night."

"A train, why not fly?"

"Um, I don't like flying, did it once and was sick the whole time. I swore I would never fly again in my life."

Charity was shocked. "I've known you all my life but I never knew that. Please forgive me, Jess."

"Nothing to forgive, honey. You were just a kid then. I'll go tell Daniel that he's in charge while I'm gone."

The next day Daniel and Jess spent most of the day together. Jess knew that Daniel would do a good job.

"Can I drive you there?" Charity asked when he was about to leave. Jess looked at her paused a moment and grinned, "Do you think I'd have it any other way?"

On the way to the train depot Jess figured this was the right time to have his talk. He took a deep breath and then blurted out,

"Charity, you know I hired Daniel to train him to take over for me, right? I think this wedding was all part of God's perfect timing. I'm ready to retire, but I was wondering if you would let me stay on in the bunkhouse? I have money saved up, but I don't want to leave." Charity glanced over trying not to cry, "I don't want you to leave either, Jess. Of course you can stay here, but why the bunkhouse?"

"Why not stay where you are?" Charity questioned Jess.

"Because Daniel will need the rooms. We made do with as we are now because we knew it would only be for the time that I was training him."

"I asked all the men before I hired Daniel and no one wanted to take over, they all like what they are doing."

"Jess, this is your home, it always will be I hope," Charity told him.

At the depot Charity and Jess hugged. "See you in a week, please come home," she said. He boarded the train, found a seat and then looked out the window and waved.

His niece and her fiancé met him at the station. *Looks to be a decent man*, he thought.

The first thing he noticed at his sisters was that things were as hectic here on Sunday mornings as it was at home. The dress rehearsal was set for the next evening and the wedding the day after that. Katrina and Doug seemed well suited; they had met at the annual convention for dentists last year. Doug had moved into town because they were opening a dental practice together. He decided to ask her to marry him so that while the office was being remodeled, they would have time for a honeymoon. Lisa, his sister, was so excited; they had plenty of things to keep them busy for the next two days making all the final arrangements.

Today they had all the last minute things to be done for a wedding, Jess was ready to go home just thinking of everything needing to be done.

Life was sure slower at home, he thought. When it was time to go home Jess and the honeymooners boarded the train, seems that Katrina didn't like to fly either.

Jess spied Daniel on the depot platform waiting for him. As they drove, Daniel updated him on a few matters. When they arrived, Charity was waiting at the gate, eager to see Jess again. Daniel and Todd had moved all of Jess's things to the bunkhouse as they had discussed the day before he left.

Simon was waiting in the bunkhouse as Jess walked in, eager to see his old friend. After settling in, he pulled out the checkerboard.

"Oh it's so good to be home!" Jess exclaimed.

CHAPTER 13

Daniel went to talk to Jess the day after he got home.

"Jess, I have a favor to ask of you."

"What's that, Daniel?"

"Well, I know you are retired, but can I impose upon you to take over while my in-laws and son are here? They will be here in just over two week's time."

"Of course I will, Daniel"—he squeezed his shoulders—"and don't feel as though you are imposing. Truth be told, I am kind of bored. I thought I was ready for retirement but…" he stopped right there and looked back at Daniel and smiled.

"Thanks Jess that's a big relief." Daniel turned to face Simon and asked him, "What are you going to need for this last group?"

"Nothing out of the ordinary," Simon replied. "Jess was wondering though if you would be supervising the activities we have for children, seeing as how it's your kid and all?"

Daniel nodded. "You two don't have to worry about Josiah. I'll be spending all my time with him, but would you two mind if he came in here? He loves to play checkers and who else but you two would be better to play with him and keep an eye on him, I need to spend some time with the in-laws, too. I need to discuss his future and feel them out about about me taking him back full-time in the near future."

"I think that is a good idea, Daniel. A boy needs his father, and that isn't to say that his grandparents aren't giving him all that but as I found out this past week, being older you tend to get tired faster than a younger person."

━╱▚━

Charity was getting nervous—it was only two weeks before Daniel's son and in-laws would arrive. *Why is that Lord?* Out in the barn Daniel was asking the same thing.

Charity walked to the bunkhouse looking for Jess. When she went in though, he was not there. Simon told her he was in the office with Daniel. As she headed over to the barn, she thought maybe riding would do her some good, so she decided to do it. Instead of asking Jess to go with her, she just saddled up Sarah and took off. The further she got from the house, the better she felt. But the next thing she knew it was getting dark, and Sarah started acting strange. She heard it first—a rattling noise. Then she saw what it was—a Diamondback rattlesnake— and it was irritated. She tried to calm Sarah down but she wasn't having it. She went wild all of a sudden, and Charity lost her balance and fell off. As she landed she tried to break her fall with her arms, she heard it snap.

"Great the one time I didn't tell anyone where I was going and now this," Charity said out loud. To top it off Sarah had run off. She heaved a sigh but managed to stay calm despite the gravity of the situation.

An hour later, Charity was hurting, her leg, and her hand too; but mostly, it was her pride as she headed back towards the ranch on foot. She just hoped that Sarah had made it back to the barn and someone noticed her saddled but riderless and would come looking for her. As another hour went by, she could just see the outlines of the line shack on her south pasture.

"Ah good I need to rest," she told herself.

As she got closer to the shack, she saw a horse and rider coming towards her—it was Daniel.

"Yeah, somebody found me!"

As Daniel got closer however, she noticed he looked angry. *Now why would he be angry*, she thought.

Daniel rode up to Charity, jumped off his horse, and kept coming, yelling at her the whole time.

"How could you run off like that and not tell someone where you were going?" he shouted. "You know better than that, I ought to take you over my knee and give you the spanking you deserve."

Charity stared up at him, still clueless why he was upset. "Why are you mad at me?" she wailed. "Aren't you the one who told me I should start riding again? Well I did and now I broke my hand, my leg hurts, and all you can think of is yelling at me?"

At that, Daniel finally noticed that her limping was more pronounced, and that she was cradling her hand so and he stopped short "Are you okay?"

"No I'm not, as I said my arm hurts, my leg hurts but mostly my pride," she whispered the last word, almost in tears. "I can't believe I couldn't hold on."

Daniel calmed down. "When I saw Sarah coming running in and no rider on her I panicked, don't ever do that to me again. Simon said you had come looking for Jess. Why didn't you tell us you wanted to ride?"

"I just wanted to escape. I was getting nervous just thinking of Josiah and your in-laws coming, so I thought that it would calm me down, and it did until that stupid ole rattler decided we had invaded his territory."

Daniel then picked her up, put her on his horse, and got on himself. "Okay, fine. Just don't do something that stupid again," he paused, "unless you like me worrying?"

"You were worried?"

"Yes."

"I kind of like hearing that Daniel." All Daniel could do was grumph at that.

When they arrived at the barn, she saw all the hands were waiting around the corral. When they saw her though, they knew she was okay and started heading in for dinner. They could wait to hear the story during supper, which thankfully Simon had stepped in and made while she was gone. Charity promised to let someone know where she was at all times, but it felt good to have someone to love and care for her. After dinner, Daniel drove her to the ER to have her checked out.

They did an X-ray on her hand and leg. The leg was fine but her hand had a hairline fracture. They gave her a prescription for a hand glove and some painkillers. She was to wear the glove at all times for the next month but that it should not stop her from doing her normal things.

The next two weeks flew by. Daniel announced at dinner that evening that as of tomorrow morning Jess would be in charge.

"My son is arriving. I'll be taking my vacation this year as a guest here."

Then Jess stood up. "As to the rest of you, Todd and Roger, you will be leading the group this time. As you know this will be the last group of the year. I hope you have enjoyed all the help we have gotten out of them this summer, so let's show these folks what real cowboy work is."

Daniel smiled just thinking of the fun that he would be having spending time with Josiah at the ranch.

CHAPTER 14

Charity greeted the new group of clients the next morning; that was usually the extent of her contact with them; Simon would be their cook and Todd would be their guide. She had asked Daniel beforehand if he would be eating with the group or still at the house with her and Jess. He had told her he would love dining with them, if she didn't mind having Josiah too. Charity smiled.

"I would be honored to have him eat with us. Do you think your in-laws will mind?"

"Doesn't matter if they do or not," Daniel replied. "Besides, this is my time to spend with him."

Charity nodded. "Do you know what his favorite foods are? I would like to make them the first night he arrives."

Daniel smiled. "Macaroni and cheese with hot dogs."

"Then that is what we will have." She grinned.

Since dinner would be simple that night, Charity went down to the barn that afternoon to take Sarah for a ride. Actually, she had seen Daniel in the corral with Josiah and just wanted to be closer to him.

Thank you God for sending him here, she thought. When she got close, Daniel called out to her. "I was just asking Josiah if he wanted to go for a ride. Wanna come along?"

"Yes please!" *That is what I was coming out here to do in the first place.*

"Let's get going then. I'll saddle Sarah if you want to hold Brody for me, that way Josiah doesn't have to get down."

Daniel left his son with Charity and saddled up Sarah for her. It took him all of a few minutes—he was that excited to go riding with them both.

Just seeing them together brought him joy. *She would make a good mother.* Just then a vision of a little girl with green eyes came to him and Josiah was holding her. *That is my wish Lord*, Daniel prayed.

The ride lasted an hour. Since Josiah wasn't used to riding, they couldn't gallop and race as they had been doing for the last two weeks, but Charity understood. She prayed that one day he would be able to ride along side them and race with them. Josiah was having so much fun being on the ranch.

"Yahoo!" he shouted when they walked into the kitchen. "Mac and cheese with dogs, my favorite!" Charity and Jess just smiled.

"And chocolate cake too for our dessert," Jess said.

Josiah looked up to his dad "I like this place, Dad. Can I live here too?"

Daniel chuckled. "Well, son, we'll just have to see if that can be done."

Charity silently prayed that it would happen too, because after just one day with Josiah, she felt drawn to him already. Daniel knew that by the end of this week he would have to talk with the Childs. Just seeing Josiah here was proof that he needed to take a more active part in raising his son.

On Tuesday, Charity went to her prison ministry meeting. Pastor Mark pulled her aside before the meeting and told her that Nathaniel would like to speak to her.

"About what?" she queried.

"Something personal is all he told me when I came to visit with him last Saturday."

"What time are visiting hours?"

"Eight to five on Saturdays and one to six on Sundays," he replied.

"Thank you, Pastor, for telling me. I'll pray about it."

After the meeting, Mrs. Davis approached her and told her the same thing. "I go on Sunday afternoons. If you want to go just let me know, and I'll go on Saturday. Nathaniel seemed serious about this."

"As I told Pastor Mark, I'll pray about it this week. I'll let you both know on Friday what I have decided."

She went home to pray about it she also wanted to talk to Daniel about it. So the next morning during breakfast she asked him, "Do you have some time to meet with me later to discuss something I need your advice on?" "Sure no problem, I'll either be in the office or the corral for most of today." "Thanks Daniel, I really appreciate it." Josiah looked up from his plate and reminded his dad, "Don't forget you promised me that I could go riding today." "I haven't forgotten son, now finish up your breakfast so Miss Charity can get some work done" Once the meal was over they headed out to the barn to begin their day and give her some time to get some work done also. Just before lunch she headed out to the barn to look for Daniel, she found him in the office so she asked, "Is this a good time?" Daniel looked up as she walked in, "Yes it is, so what is it that you would like my advice on Charity? "Pastor Mark and Mrs. Davis both passed along a message from Nathaniel about wanting to speak to me. Before you ask, they don't know what about because I already asked. Daniel I don't know if I am ready for a personal meeting with him, Should I go?" "Have you prayed about it?" (he asked as he reached over the desk to place his hand over hers.) "Yes I did, deep down I know I should, however I'm a little afraid to go."

"I'll go with you if you wish," he told her. (as he gave her hand another little squeeze)

"Thanks, but I should do this on my own if I do go," she said and changed the topic. "Will you be going to choir rehearsal?"

"Yes, I've already asked my in-laws and Jess to entertain him that night until we get home. By the way, my in-laws are very impressed with the ranch and this program. She said the ranch hands must really love your family for doing this for you while you were in the hospital." Charity hiccupped as she responds,

"Oh, Daniel, that means so much to me. For a long time I was so mad at God, I didn't even appreciate what they had done. I'm just so thankful that they did though."

"Losing this place would've just killed me; all my memories would be gone." She was almost on the verge of sobbing as Daniel spoke up,

"You're wrong about that, Charity. You'll always have your memories no matter where you end up at in life." Another hiccupped breath snuck out before she could respond,

"I know but losing this place would've just been that much harder to accept, after losing my family."

━╱╲━

That evening Amy called her, all excited.

"Guess what, Charity? Tell Daniel that he can bring Josiah to choir rehearsal tomorrow night if he wants."

"Why? There is no child care."

"There is now! Bruce was asked to join the choir tonight, and I offered to do child care just so we could be together since I can't sing. Pastor Mark said there were several people in the choir that would be happy to have child care offered."

"I'll go tell him now. He had already asked his in-laws to entertain him but I'm sure he would rather have him come with us."

She quickly hung up the phone and went out to the corral where Daniel was walking Star on the lead rope with Josiah sitting atop her. Sarah was walking beside them, keeping her calm. She entered the corral, stroked Sarah's head, and gave her an apple. She saved one piece for Star, too.

"Sarah you are such a good girl, do you mind that Josiah is riding Star instead of you? Maybe next time Daniel will put Josiah on you." She turned to Star stroked the neck, "And what did you do to have received the honor of carrying Josiah today?

Josiah turned to his dad and asked, "Why does she talk to them?"

115

Charity smiled. "I have always talked to them since the day they were both born. My daddy used to tell me that they need love and attention too, just like we do." Sarah neighed and nodded her head as if in agreement.

Josiah seemed thoughtful. "Can I feed and talk to them too?"

"Only with me around, son," Daniel answered.

Then Charity turned to Daniel and told him what Amy has just told her. Daniel grinned as he asked, "Can I trust her?"

Charity playfully swatted his arm. "This will be great practice for her, their child is due in a couple of months."

"What about it Josiah want to come with Daddy and Miss Charity to church tomorrow night?"

"Will they have milk and cookies there? Jess promised me we would have them while you are gone."

Charity shrugged her shoulders and giggled. "I can bring some if you want, Daniel. Or you can leave him home, it's up to you."

He turned to his son, "Seems as if you will get some at either place, so what do you want to do, son?"

"I want to go with you, Daddy."

"It's settled then, you are coming with us," Daniel said.

Charity headed for the door. "I'll let Jess know at suppertime."

In the mean time, Charity went inside and baked a batch of chocolate chip cookies to bring to church.

As they were leaving for choir practice, she grabbed a gallon of milk and added some plastic cups to the bag with the cookies. That night Amy had just two children, but a few parents said that next week they would bring theirs too. Each parent said they would like to take turns bringing snacks also. Amy had already volunteered to bring them the next week though and would set up a schedule for the parents to know when it was their turn.

Friday morning came and Charity had made her decision. She would go visit Nathaniel tomorrow afternoon, so she called the Pastor to him know what time she would be going.

"Now I need to call Mrs. Davis and let her know too."

"She's here now so I'll tell her for you," the pastor said.

CHAPTER 15

On Saturday afternoon, Charity was at the prison by two. Nathaniel came into the visiting room and thanked her for coming.

They chose one of the tables as far away from the vending machines and all the other visitors as much as was possible in the crowded room, "I don't know if you know it, Charity," Nathaniel started. "But I was sentenced to eight years. The warden told me though that sometime next year I would be eligible for an early release due to my good behavior. I intend on coming to church there and getting involved with the prison ministry and just wanted to know if you would be okay with that."

"Nathaniel, I told you I forgave you just as God has," Charity held his hands, "I know you didn't mean for it to happen, and I realize now that maybe it had to happen to get you to come to know God. Thankfully you did, your grandmother is so happy. Have you told your parents yet?"

"Yes, mom came earlier today and I told her. Gram says that mom is thinking of attending also. I hope she does and someday my dad will too."

"Yes, your grandmother has told me a little about your mom, and I've added your parents to my prayer list. Something good will come of all of this, of that I am sure. God promises us that."

Nathaniel was delighted and wasn't able to mask it. "The warden has already noted in my file that I would be allowed to come back with the committee and be involved with the prison's Bible study. I should be finished with my online courses by then, and Pastor Mark has agreed to sponsor me in furthering my studies."

The guards announced that her visiting time was over, so she said good-bye to Nathaniel and left.

On Sunday morning after breakfast, they left for church once they arrived it dawned on her that she had forgotten to plug in the crock pot which was to be their dinner, she quickly pulled out her cell to call the bunkhouse to ask one of the men to run up to the house and plug it in for her. After church, Mrs. Davis stopped her, "How did it go with Nathaniel yesterday?"

"Oh fine," Charity answered. "He just wanted to let me know that next year he is eligible for an early release and wanted to make sure I would be okay with him attending church here. I told him it wouldn't bother me at all. He also told me his mom knows and just as you thought, she is thinking of attending also." Mrs. Davis and Charity joined hands and took a moment to pray that her son and daughter-in-law would actually start attending church.

Daniel came by at that moment and asked, "Ready to go?"

"Yes." She looked down at Josiah. "Are you up for riding after supper?"

Josiah gave a miniature smile of Daniel and gave the thumbs up sign, and then she got the same exact smile from Daniel. She ruffled his hair. "Okay then, Josiah. Let's go home and eat so we can go riding."

After an hour of riding Charity noticed that Josiah was nodding. She rode up beside Daniel and whispered, "I think we have a little boy who's ready for his nap."

"Okay," Daniel looked down, "time's up for today young man."

As they rode up Jess was waiting at the corral. He looked really concerned.

"Daniel we've got a problem! Thunder has disappeared, I didn't see any broken fences but he's not in the pasture. I asked Todd if one of the hands or guests had seen anything while out riding," he paused for a moment, apparently breathless for he babbled too fast. "We need to find that bull. I'll be right with you as soon as I can."

Daniel then turned to Charity. "Can you watch him while I go help look?"

"Of course," she said and held Josiah's arms. "Come on Josiah lets go up to the house and wait for your Dad."

Within a few minutes, she had unsaddled Sarah and they walked to the house. She tucked him in her brother's room and read him a story until he fell asleep.

Daniel and some of the men rode out to the pasture where Thunder should've been. Jess was right about no broken fences, but he did notice that one section looked newer than the others and went to investigate. When he got up close, he noticed a piece of lead rope on the ground. He looked around and saw some kind of vehicle tracks, so he shouted out to the closest hands to find Jess and bring him here. Within ten minutes they returned with Jess, he rode up hard and fast.

"What's up Daniel?" he asked as he got off his horse.

"Look closely Jess and tell me exactly what you see."

"Well…….right off I can see this section of fence is newer than the rest, which we haven't done here lately."

"And upon closer inspection, I also see a piece of lead rope and tracks of some kind." Then Jess asked, "Where's Todd? Maybe he ordered it done."

Jess turned to Chester. "Go find Todd and ask if he recently ordered this section of the fence to be redone, if not then call the sheriff. We have a rustling problem and tell him where he can find us." Chester took off. Todd rode up in another ten minutes.

"No I didn't order any fencing repairs out here, so Chester is calling the sheriff."

"We need to have the men ride the fence lines and check in the other pastures to see if they got anything else," Daniel said. He told the hands standing around which direction they should go check, he sent Todd back to the bunkhouse to get the rest of the hands and the guests "No guests are to check fences without a regular hand being with them," he turned to Jess, "who here knows all her property besides you?"

"Randy," he replied and called out to him, "Randy, come here."

"Since you know the property will you come with me to follow the tracks?" Daniel said when Randy got up to them.

"Yes," he agreed.

Daniel turned to Jess. "Will you wait here for the sheriff?"

"Sure thing."

Daniel checked to see if he had a signal to call Charity and let her know, luckily in this section of the property he did.

Charity was looking outside the kitchen window watching Todd ride up and run into the bunkhouse when her cell phone rang. Seeing the caller ID she answered right away.

"Daniel what's going on? I just saw Todd come riding in fast and going into the bunk house. Is anyone hurt?"

"No. No one is hurt but we have a rustling problem, seems as if they took Thunder. The men will ride the fence lines and see if they got anything else. Randy and I are going to follow the tracks and Jess will wait here for the sheriff,"

"Can you please keep an eye on Josiah, I have no idea how long we'll be out here." He asked as he and Randy were mounted and already following the tracks the rustlers had left.

"Of course, Daniel," she said softly. "No problem, I understand, don't worry about Josiah, I'll make sure he's okay just get going and follow them before it's too late."

Another hour went by and the Sheriff finally arrived at the house. Todd escorted him out to the pasture. When they got to where Jess was, they dismounted and went to hear what they had found. Sheriff Joe Casey, the town's new sheriff of six months, hadn't had the time to meet everyone yet, so they introduced themselves and then Jess briefed him on what they had found and what Daniel and Randy were doing. At that point, some of the hands rode up giving reports as to what they had found in their sections. They then rode to the other sections and let them know to meet back at the barn to give their reports to the Sheriff, as he needed to go back and grab his samples kit.

As the rest of the teams came back, they all had negative reports. They now knew that they had only gotten away with the bull. Todd and Sheriff Joe were going back. Charity knew how far they would need to ride after that to reach a road, so she packed some food for them. Joe took his samples kit to make a mold of the tire tracks.

After Vicki and Josh returned from their searching, Vicki went looking for Charity.

"We can take care of him if you have something you need to do."

"You can keep us company," Charity replied. "It's going to be a long night, I'm afraid."

Josh and Vicki spent the evening entertaining their grandson and Charity. Jess stayed in the bunkhouse with the other hands waiting, just in case they could help. Sheriff Joe made his mold of the tire tracks quickly then they jumped back over the fence and headed so he could get it back to headquarters to be kept safe until he needed it later.

In the meantime, Daniel and Randy had been following the tracks—it was leading them over the mountain range to the main highway. Daniel called the bunkhouse but was told that the sheriff and Todd had already left to return to the pasture, so he called Todd on his cell to tell him which way the tracks were heading. Sheriff Joe then called it in to the station to put out an APB (an All Points Bulletin) for a truck and trailer with a bull in it.

They were at that point already on the way back to the ranch so he could get his car and head in that direction. As they came in Todd went to update Jess, and Sheriff

Joe left. Charity heard the noise of his siren and came running out. Jess was just walking up the path to give her the update.

When Daniel and Randy reached the top of the mountain range, they saw a truck pulling a trailer entering the highway. So he called the house and updated Jess on which direction they went. Jess immediately called the sheriff's station and reported what Daniel had seen. They put out another APB on which direction they were going. Joe heard it and as he was already in that area, continued his search.

Jess told Charity everything and that Daniel and Randy were heading back since they had no chance of catching up to them on horses. Just as Daniel and Randy rode up the phone rang, Jess ran inside the barn to answer it. It was Sheriff Joe.

"We found them at Macy's café, care to come and get your prize bull?"

"I'll get a truck and trailer together immediately," Jess answered. "And it should take about two hours to get there." He hung up the phone and called out to the nearest hand.

"Hook up the trailer to the truck immediately the bull has been found."

Daniel was just unsaddling and overheard the order.

"Where?" he asked.

"In the parking lot of Macy's cafe, apparently they got hungry and stopped to eat."

Charity had walked out to the barn when she saw that Daniel had ridden in and overheard Jess.

"I am coming too," she said. She ran back up to the house where Josiah and his grandparents were waiting, The Childs' volunteered to watch Josiah so that she could ride along with Daniel, they offered to stay overnight with Josiah. She let them know where they could sleep and where fresh towels were and grabbed some food for Daniel as the truck arrived at the front door.

They headed out towards town and then the highway. Daniel decided to discuss with Charity the idea of Josiah coming to live with him.

"Charity do you think it's a good idea to have Josiah come live with me full time?"

"Are you ready for it?" she asked.

"I think I am but what about child care. And how can I get him to school and back while I am working for you?"

"I could do it," she replied, "That is, if you trust me."

"I do trust you but that is a big commitment."

"I know it is, Daniel. But I would love to have a chance at it."

"What do you think Josh and Vicki will think?"

"That's just it I don't have any idea what they are going to think."

"Have you prayed about this, Daniel?"

"Yes I have, and I believe that God is putting this on my heart to go forward. I panicked when Victoria died and didn't want to even think of raising a child by myself at the time."

"Did you tell them it would be for a little while or permanently?"

"I think I told them permanently, but I don't really remember."

"All you can do is to be sure that this is what God is leading you to do and then just go speak with them about it. They seem to be nice people to me. I'm sure they will understand once you explain it to them"—Charity looked into his eyes and held his gaze—"I'll pray for you to receive clarification from the Lord."

Daniel smiled. "That's good to know, and I have watched you over the past couple of years and have seen how you have changed your attitude towards God and how your faith has been restored."

"Thank you, Daniel. I was pretty mad when I finally came out of the coma, even though I was angry at him I could always feel that he was near me. I really think that I felt everyone's prayers although I refused to admit it to anyone until now," she looked away for a moment, reluctant to continue but she did anyway. "I believe that God sent you here to help restore my faith."

"Wow, Charity that's very humbling to know that he could use me. A man who turned away from him because I felt I had failed him somehow."

"Daniel, we only fool ourselves, God knows what is deep inside us and waits for us to notice it and turn back to him, and HE never fails." "Amen to that" he replied.

As they pulled into the diner, and Sheriff Joe walked out, Charity introduced him to Daniel.

"That was sure some fast thinking on your part, Daniel," Sheriff Joe commented. "We might not have caught them without it. They were just getting back into their truck when I saw them. If you had waited for me to arrive, we wouldn't have known which direction to head. Good thing I'm the law though because I can tell you not once was I doing the speed limit." They all laughed at that.

Three hours later they came rolling back into the yard, several hands were there waiting to unload Thunder and take him back to his pasture. Daniel and Charity walked into the kitchen. Jess had already made them a pot of coffee and some breakfast. A new day was dawning.

CHAPTER 16

On Monday both Daniel and Charity hoped to find time to take a short nap. That evening she would make all of Daniel's favorite foods; she was so grateful for his fast thinking, without it she could have lost her prize bull. She would also make the men's favorite desserts and send them down to the bunkhouse because without them and the guests, it would've taken a lot longer and possibly never to find the rustlers.

Josiah woke up all happy to see his daddy, when it was his time for a nap, Daniel decided to take one with him. Charity was passing the room she saw them together. *What a beautiful sight that was*, she thought. As she headed off to her room to grab a quick nap also.

Daniel was on his way to talk with his in-laws but stopped at the bunkhouse first to let Simon and Todd know that the Childs would not be a part of the daily activities tomorrow, he needed some time to speak to them about an important matter.

"What?" Simon asked.

"I want Josiah to come live with me permanently, Charity and I worked out all the details while we went to go get Thunder."

Todd slapped him on the back. "Good for you, a boy needs his daddy."

Simon nodded his hand and said the same thing. Daniel then headed towards the guest cabins to request his in-laws to stay behind tomorrow because he wanted to discuss Josiah's future with them.

Vicki turned towards her husband and said, "Do you think he's finally going to take him?"

Josh grabbed her hands and replied, "Honey I hope so. It's time they are together."

If only Daniel had heard, he wouldn't have had such a sleepless night.

Tuesday after breakfast, Josh went to tell Todd not to expect them for the day's activity.

He told them "Yeah I know, Daniel told me last night."

"Do you think he's ready to take Josiah now?" Vicki asked.

Todd smiled. "You need to talk to him about that, Mrs. Childs."

"Honey by the smile on Todd's face I do believe he is. We can only pray he is and make that boy the happiest little man around," Josh said.

After breakfast, Daniel stayed in the house with Josiah and Charity waiting for his in-laws and praying they would say yes. At the sound of knocking, he jumped up so quickly that he knocked his chair over.

"Sit down, Daniel," Charity said. "I'll answer the door." She walked to the door and opened it, "Come in, we're still at the breakfast table."

"Did we come too early?" Vicki asked.

"No we are finished, he's just sitting there waiting, all nervous but don't tell him I told you so"—she winked and smiled—"follow me."

Daniel took a steadying breath and prepared himself.

"Would either of you like a cup of coffee?" Charity asked them as they entered the kitchen.

"Yes," all three adults answered, so she poured everyone a cup and turned her attention to Josiah.

"Josiah how would you like to go with me to give Sarah and Star an apple or a sugar cube?"

"That would be great!" he replied.

Charity told him to grab a couple of sugar cubes off the table.

Josiah can't contain his excitement. "I would be feeding Sarah, her mommy, and Star would take them right out of my pocket."

They left and Daniel gulped. *Okay this is it*, he thought.

"I asked you here today—" he began as Vicki started to talk at the same time.

"Are you ready to?"

They all laughed and Daniel breathed a sigh of relief.

"You go first Vicki."

"We're hoping that you are finally ready to raise your son."

He blinked. "Yes," he sputtered. "That's why I wanted to talk to you."

Josh smiled. "Well this is going the way we hoped it would, Daniel. That little boy needs you. We are good substitutes but he needs his daddy. We have been praying for over a year that you would be ready. That's really the reason why we decided to come here this year."

Daniel got up and hugged them both. "You've made me the happiest man on earth. Truthfully, I didn't know how to approach you about it. I couldn't remember if I had told you it would be for a little while or if I had told you permanently."

"You did tell us permanently, but we had always hoped it would only be for awhile," Vicki chimed in. "We could see how much you loved him even then, but we also saw the panic in your eyes so we agreed."

"Do you mind if I call Charity to have her bring Josiah back?" Daniel asked.

"By all means," they replied.

Daniel quickly pulled out his cell and called the stables. After a few rings, Charity answered. "Paradise Ranch, how may I help you?"

"Charity, it's Daniel. Can you please bring Josiah to the house?"

"Right away, Daniel" She hung up and called out to him. "Josiah, your daddy wants to talk to you so let's go back."

"But I'm still feeding Star," Josiah replied.

"That's okay we can come back later and you can finish."

He ran towards her then and they walked back to the kitchen, swinging their arms as they walked.

Charity prayed as they walked back to the house that it had gone well. They hadn't been gone very long. Once they entered the kitchen and Charity could see that it had gone well, all the adults were smiling. She quietly left them all alone and went upstairs to make the beds, thanking God as she did her chores for such a favorable response.

Daniel hollered up the stairs. "Charity, can you come down?"

"I'm coming." Daniel grabbed her up when she reached the bottom step and swung her in a circle. She laughed and replied, "It must have gone well."

"Yes, it did. In fact, that's the reason they came here this year to talk to me about it."

"What do I need to do to get him enrolled?" Charity asked. "Can you put me down at least, although I *do* like it."

She blushed because she had said that aloud. Daniel replied, "If I have to, but I like having you in my arms." He also blushed when he said that.

"So tell me," Daniel said. "All I do know is that you will need his immunization records. I can call the school for you and find out what else."

"Do you think you could do that today? I don't even know where the school is, let alone the name and number."

Charity laughed. "Don't worry, Daniel, I can take care of it."

Daniel said, "Oh, I forgot to say that they gave me all his records already."

"Well, at least we are one step ahead in the process," Charity said.

She got out her telephone book, looked up the number to the school, picked up the phone, and dialed the school immediately. She asked whomever answered the phone what was needed to enroll a child.

"For a kindergartner, you only need a birth certificate, proof of residency, and immunization records."

Charity said, "Thank very much. Is it too late to sign him up?"

"No." She had written it all down so Daniel would know right then.

He said, "Thank you, Charity. I'll go ask Vicki if she brought his birth certificate right now. I'll be right back." Daniel raced out to the guest cabins to ask Vicki.

When Daniel returned, he had in his hands the documents he needed. "Can we go to register him today? I know it's getting close to school starting."

"Yes, Daniel, we can go right now if you wish."

"Yes, please. That way, I can get everything done today and not have to ask Jess to take over for another day too. Although I do know he loves it."

Charity smiled. "Jess will always volunteer to help others."

They cleaned up the coffee cups and got ready to go into town.

At the school, they walked into the office, and Charity asked the girl, "What forms do we need to fill out to register a child?"

She was handed a clipboard with several forms on it. They sat down and began filling them out. The young girl asked if they would mind if she took Josiah to the playground while they were finishing up with the forms and talking with the vice principal.

"She'll give you a tour of the school and bring you to the playground at the end."

"Yes, that would be fine," Daniel responded.

She introduced them to the vice principal, Mrs. Cotter, who invited them to come into her office and finish filling out the forms.

"Normally, we also introduce you to the principal, Mr. Spencer, but he's out sick today." Charity responded, "Oh, we know him. We attend the same church."

Daniel asked Charity, "Is that the Mr. Spencer in the choir?"

"Yes, Daniel, it is."

When they had finished with the forms and the classroom tour, they went to the playground to get Josiah. "Dad, this place is awesome. They have a better playground than the school by Grandma's house."

Daniel ruffled Josiah's hair and said, "It's time to go, son."

"Okay, do we get to go riding when we get home?"

"Yes." Daniel turned to Mrs. Cotter and thanked her for everything, shook her hand, and they left.

When they got back to the ranch, Daniel put all Josiah's paperwork away and then said, "Any one up for a ride, or should we have lunch first?"

Josiah quickly answered, "I want to go riding first." He turned to Charity. "Are you coming too?"

"Yes." She walked out of the office and over to the stall where Sarah was. "Are you up for a ride too?"

Sarah nodded her head and nickered. Then she went to Star's stall, and she was already hanging her head over the fence to receive her sugar cube and her love. Daniel told Josiah to go wait on the stump while he saddled up Star for him and Red, his horse. In the meantime, Charity was saddling up Sarah.

After an hour or so, they decided they were hungry, and so they headed back to the ranch for a late lunch.

CHAPTER 17

Daniel and Josiah excused themselves and Charity went to do the dishes and got supper going. Then the phone rang, it was Cindy.

"Charity I was wondering if you and I could get together."

"Sure Cindy! Now or is lunch tomorrow at the diner okay?"

"Tomorrow will be fine."

Charity finished getting supper ready and wondered what Cindy wanted to talk to her about. That afternoon was her prison ministry meeting, so she excused herself to get ready to leave while Jess and Daniel cleaned up the dishes. She left a little early hoping to stop at the store to see if Cindy was still working, she wasn't so she went on to her meeting.

I guess I'll just have to wait, she thought.

Wednesday morning, she announced that she would be having lunch in town with Cindy and that the hands are on their own.

"Looks like we will be eating at the bunkhouse, Daniel." Jess replied.

Daniel winked at Charity. "Tell her I said hi."

Charity laughed at that because she had already told him that Cindy thought he was *all* that. As she drove into town, she prayed that there was nothing seriously wrong with her friend.

Amy saw her the minute she entered the diner.

"Back here, Charity I have a booth saved for you two," she called out.

Charity wondered how she knew as she walked up to her. Amy smiled and said, "Before you ask no I am not physic. Cindy and I were together when she called."

Charity smiled. "I should've known, your diner is the gossip place in town."

"I resent that." Amy laughed.

"I don't gossip Charity Stewart."

"Amy, I didn't say you gossip, I said this place is the gossip center."

"Do you know why she wants to talk?"

"No, but she called in your orders so it will be ready when she gets here so it must be something good." Just then, Cindy walked in and saw them.

"As always Amy, perfect timing. Thank you." Cindy sat down and said, "What do you know about Sheriff Joe? Sorry I'm so abrupt, but I'm on my lunch hour."

"Not much, why?"

Because I think he is a dream. Even better than your Daniel, but I don't know how to get his attention."

"Aha, so that's what this is all about. How about I invite him to dinner to thank him for his quick capture of Thunder and coincidently have forgotten I had invited you for dinner?"

"Do you think it will work?"

"Never know until we try, Cindy."

"Okay you let me know and in the meantime how is that dreamboat of yours? I saw him in church with a little boy that had a miniature smile like his in his arms. What is that about?"

"Oh! Josiah is his son who has been living with his grandparents, and they decided to bring him here for Daniel's vacation instead of him going there. They also wanted to see if Daniel would be ready to take him back and raise him. Yesterday we went to the school and enrolled him for kindergarten. By all that, you know he is ready and now you know everything and thanks for ordering my lunch Cindy."

Then they got down to enjoying their food.

Amy brought them dessert and asked, "Okay, girls. What is this about? If you can tell me."

Cindy grinned. "Charity has agreed to have Sheriff Joe over for dinner and introduce me to him."

Amy smiled. "Love is definitely in the air this year. Has he agreed?"

"Hold on a minute and we'll know," Charity said as she dialed the Sheriff's office on speaker phone and asked for him. They put her through and she invited him to dinner Friday night if he could make it around seven o'clock.

"Sure I will as long as there are no emergencies," he answered her.

"Let me see what I can do about that Sheriff," Charity responded.

He laughed. "I wish it was that easy, Ms. Stewart."

"Oh my gosh! I need to buy a new dress." Cindy said after Charity hung up.

Amy and Charity just smiled.

"Amy, pregnancy becomes you," Charity told her. "When is your due date?"

"Two more months," Amy replied.

"Are you going to find out the sex or wait?"

"We've decided to wait. Whatever the Lord has for us we will be happy, and I'm so thankful I didn't have any morning sickness during my pregnancy."

"Have you and Bruce decided on names?"

"Not entirely. If it's a girl we like Miranda. We aren't sure if it's a boy, I like his Dad's name David but he likes Stephen. I hope that won't bother you?"

"Not at all! It would be an honor to my brother, but I don't want it to always be a reminder to you of the accident."

"Charity, he wants to do it because he says that it was only Stephen's death that allowed us to meet."

"Well…whatever you decide. I'll love the child no matter what, after all you are my sister."

Then she paid the bill and left. On the way home Charity prayed that Cindy and the Sheriff would hit it off and that Amy would have a healthy baby.

When she got home, she went out to the corral and told Daniel about the lunch and the plans she had made for Friday night.

"Does that mean I am not all that anymore?" Daniel responded playfully.

"No, actually," Charity responded. "She is now calling you my dreamboat, said she saw you and Josiah in church Sunday and thinks you have the cutest son. Too bad he is so young." Daniel laughed aloud and put his arm around her. "Am I your dreamboat?"

"For today," she said, flipping her hair behind her face and smiling saucily. "Daniel, there is only a few more days until this set of guests leave. Do you need to go back with them and get all his things?"

"Yes, I will. I was just thinking of that this afternoon. Do you think you can get away and come with me?"

"Yes, if that is what you want. I can ask Jess to manage things while we are gone."

"No need, I'll ask him as I am the foreman."

Charity swatted his arm. "Hey I am the boss you know. If I want to ask him, then I shall. Luckily for you I don't want too."

With that, she walked off and went to the house. She could hear Daniel laughing the whole way, and smiled to herself.

Thank you Lord for sending this man to me to make me smile again, she thought.

Daniel went to the bunkhouse to ask Jess, "Would you mind extending your foreman duties for a little longer? I've asked Charity to come along with me when my in-laws leave at the end of the week. I need to pick up all of Josiah's things, we should be gone about a week."

Jess patted him on the back, "Sure thing Daniel that won't be a problem at all, I'd be happy to, I'm glad things worked out." "Thank you Jess, I was hoping you would feel that way." Then Daniel headed over to the guest cabins to talk with his in-laws about what he would need to buy. After that he headed back to his rooms to make room to accommodate Josiah's things before it was time for dinner.

"Charity can we head into town to go buy a bed and dresser for Josiah and whatever else he will need, have dinner in town and go straight to choir practice after that?" Daniel asked Thursday morning.

"I don't see why not, Daniel," she responded. "Let me tell Jess so he and the men would eat in the bunkhouse." After they had lunch, they cleaned up and headed off to town.

After they bought bedroom furniture, bedding, and a few things to help it look like a little boy's room, they headed over to the diner. Amy welcomed them and sat them down in the back.

"Why are you eating here when Charity is such a good cook?" she asked.

"We came into town early to buy things for my new room," Josiah proudly announced.

"So did you get a race car bed?"

"No way! I got a bunk bed so when I go to school and make new friends I can have them sleep over! I got all cowboy stuff for my bed and my light is even cowboys!" Josiah exclaimed.

"So what do you want for dinner then little cowboy?"

"I want a hot dog and French fries, please."

"Coming right up, and what do you two want?"

"I'll take the meatloaf," Daniel said. "Charity, what would you like?"

Charity turned to Amy grinning and said, "Fried chicken, please."

They were having so much fun talking about their day it took a moment to realize Amy was standing there with their food, so she cleared her throat to interrupt them.

"No problem," Amy said when they finally noticed her. "You are my last customers, then I'm off to choir practice the same as you three."

They ate, ordered dessert, and then noticed the time.

"We had better get going or we will be late," Charity said. Amy had dropped off the check when she brought them their dessert, so Daniel paid the bill and they drove the couple of blocks to the church. Five minutes later, Amy walked in the church with her husband.

After choir practice, Charity went to pick up Josiah. Amy looked beat so she volunteered to help clean up and wait there until the rest of the parents show up.

"Do you want to go home?" she asked Amy. "Daniel and I can stay."

"No, you've had a busy day too I'm fine." Amy said. "We don't know the sex but yesterday afternoon was my doctor's appointment, we were told we're having twins."

Charity hugged her and congratulated her. "So what does Bruce think?"

"He's as overwhelmed as I am. My parents are coming to stay for the first month so I can have some help. Then Bruce's parents are coming for the second month. At least now I know why I waddle so much."

Charity was so happy for Amy. "Can I throw you a baby shower and tell people you're having twins or does everyone know already?"

"Yes you can throw me a baby shower and no one knows but you. The doctor's office staff and the pastor so far, unless Bruce has blabbed."

"Oh Amy! This is going to be such fun! Well, maybe not at first but I know you'll get used to it with no problems. I've seen you with the kids." Charity held Amy's belly and looked up. "Have you talked to the Pastor about getting a replacement for a few months afterwards?"

"Yesterday right after my appointment. We came and talked with him. Do you know of somebody available?"

"I am thinking of Cindy! She needs to get more involved."

"That's true! I'll approach her tomorrow at lunch."

Just then, both Daniel and Bruce walked in. Bruce took one look at Amy and remarked, "You look tired, honey. Can I help?"

The last parent walked in just behind the men though so she said, "No thank you, dear. Just give me a minute to put this away and we can go." Daniel turned to Josiah and asked, "What do you say to Miss Amy, son?"

Josiah looked up at her and said, "Thank you for the food, Miss Amy."

"What food Josiah?" Daniel asked. "You just ate before we got here."

"I know, and I didn't say thank you."

Daniel laughed and ruffled his son's hair "I meant for watching you just now." "Oh! Miss Amy, thank you for watching us." He grinned and turned to his Dad. "Did I do good, Daddy?"

"Yes, son. Very good! Now it's time to get you home and into bed. Tomorrow we can put all your new things up."

Charity smiled and told Amy, "I'll pick a date. Check with you to make sure it's okay with your schedule and get the invitations sent out."

Then they all went their separate ways home. Josiah once again fell asleep on the way home, so Daniel carried him into his room.

At breakfast, she reminded Daniel and Jess about having Sheriff Joe and Cindy for dinner that night.

"Looks as if you and I are a couple tonight, Josiah." Jess said.

"Sure Jess. What's a couple?"

"It just means that you and I are dinner partners tonight."

"Oh! Well, we sit together all the time. Grandma told me it means two."

"Yes a couple is two," Jess responded as he winked at Daniel and Charity.

Around four that afternoon Charity called the Sheriff's office to speak to Joe.

"Hello, Ms. Stewart," he said when they patched her through. "I assume you are calling about tonight's dinner, as it stands right now I'm still available."

"Well, Sheriff, that's good to hear. Dinner is at seven. What time can we expect to see you? Oh, by the way I invited Cindy to stay for dinner also. We are planning Amy's baby shower and we aren't finished yet, I hope you don't mind?"

"No that isn't a problem, Ms. Stewart."

"Will you please call me Charity?"

"As you wish. See you all at seven then, okay Charity?"

"Great, Sheriff! See you at six. Good-bye."

She called up Cindy right after. "Please tell me you have today off. I just told the Sheriff you were here helping me plan Amy's baby shower, and since we weren't done yet, I invited you to dinner." She didn't wait for Cindy to react. "Can you come and help me plan it?"

"Yes I'm off today. And yes, I can come over right now to help you plan it. Sounds like fun! Give me five minutes and I'm out the door."

"See you soon." Charity felt better after that, her parents raised her not to lie.

Forty minutes later Cindy arrived. "Let's get this planned out."

"Have you set a date?"

"No, I told Amy I would see what I had available and then check to see she had anything planned on that date."

"I was thinking since she is due near the middle of October to have it near the middle of September.

"With twins, she may have them a little earlier. And I wouldn't want to have the party while she is delivering."

"Twins!" Cindy exclaimed.

"Yes! She told me last night. So far it is Bruce, the Pastor, me and you now. Oh and the grandparents, too."

"Do they know what they are having?" Cindy asked.

"No, they don't, they want to be surprised. So any colors will be fine."

"I'd like to have it here. We have lots of room."

"I saw the cutest baby invitations in the catalog yesterday that would be perfect. I'll order them, how many do you think?"

"Well...I don't know, nearly everyone in town knows her because of the diner. How many do you think we should invite?"

"All of them!" Cindy replied, laughing. "What do you think about having a coed shower?"

Charity thought about it and said, "Yes, that will work. I need to talk to Bruce about furniture since they only knew about one baby until Wednesday. The guys could have a build-a-baby-room party."

"That sounds like a good idea," Cindy replied.

Charity immediately called Bruce and told him what they were thinking.

"Oh Charity, that sounds like fun!" Bruce cried. "We don't even have the first crib yet. We've been so busy we haven't had a lot of time to prepare the nursery."

"Okay then. I'll check to see what it takes to build a couple of dressers, cribs, and a changing table and get them. Can you think of anything else?"

"I think Amy would love a rocking chair"

"This is going to be so much fun, Bruce! Do you two have plans yet for sometime in the middle of September?"

"Let me check the calendar, hold on."

"Okay," Charity said." Charity waits a few minutes while Bruce went to grab the calendar. She also heard talking in the background and assumed he was checking with Amy, then she heard the fumbling noise of the receiver being picked up indicating that he was back. "Got it Charity,

"I don't see anything for the fifteenth so I asked Amy if she had anything planned she hadn't written down. She said the fifteenth would be fine she'll ink that day down for the party." The kitchen timer went off so she said good-bye to Bruce and went to check on the roast.

"Cindy, did you happen to see an invitation I could send to the men?"

Cindy thought for a moment and said, "Yes, I do remember one that would go nicely."

"Okay then order one hundred for each one then. I'll talk to Simon about cooking up something for the men's party and will you help me with our menu?"

"Okay then. I think we've done enough for one day, Joe should be arriving soon so I need to get the bread rolls in the oven." Just then the kitchen door opened and

Daniel, Jess, and Josiah came in. Two minutes later, the front doorbell rang.

"Excuse me," Charity said, and went to answer it.

"Joe, welcome to my home! We're all in the kitchen just now. Come on back, I need to get the rolls in the oven."

Charity officially introduced Cindy to him after he said his hellos to everyone else.

"Jess could you entertain the men in the living room while we set the table please?"

"Sure," he replied. "Come on guys, let's head on out."

During dinner, she presented the plans they had made about the baby shower.

"You know, that sounds like fun," Daniel said. "I've never been to a baby shower before, I always thought they were just girls' affairs, but this build-a-baby-room idea is a good."

"Simon won't have any problems with feeding us men and I know several of our boys that would love helping to make the furniture," Jess said.

Charity turned to Joe and asked, "Are you any good at carpentry?"

He nodded. "My dad builds furniture for a living and I worked with him in his shop."

"Then my next question is"—Charity paused to look at Cindy—"will you save the fifteenth of September for the party then?"

"Sounds like a fun time to me! Sure I'd love to come."

"I'll need your address," Cindy piped up. "I'm doing the invitations—the men will get their own invitations stating what to bring with them. Do you have any suggestions besides a hammer?"

"You will need planes, saws, sand paper, dowels, nails, and of course miters." He turned to Charity and asked, "Do you know where to find the wood and blueprints?"

She grinned. "From your Dad, of course!"

Everyone laughed and proceeded to finish eating. Josiah turned to his dad and said, "I think we should make a horse dad. Don't you think they would like that?"

Daniel look down at his son and smiled. "Would you help me, son?"

"Can I?" he asked with his eyes wide open.

"Of course you can!"

Josiah just leaned into his dad and hugged him.

Well it looked as though Cindy and Joe hit it off, Charity thought as she was cleaning up after the company left.

CHAPTER 18

On Saturday morning, Charity called Amy and Bruce to find out what they were thinking of.

"Bruce told me what you are planning," Amy gushed. "That is so wonderful, Charity! What a relief it is off my shoulders, I just can't seem to find the time or energy to run the diner and get other things done right now. I feel as if I am lugging around fifty pounds."

"Amy I need to know what type of wood you want—oak, ash, pine, maple? Do you want a light color or a darker wood?" Being a multi-tasker, Charity was frosting her cake while getting the answers she needed from Amy, (I hope the men will like this cake for dessert tonight.)

"Well…" she paused in thought. "I think maple would look great but Bruce is shaking his head, hold on and let me ask what he would like. Bruce honey what do you like."

"Oak!" Charity heard Bruce say in the background.

"Charity, did you hear him?"

"Yes, now I can call Mr. Casey. Thank you very much."
Perfect timing, the cake looks yummy, now I need to call Mr.
Casey.

Then she dialed Mr. Casey's number to find out what
she would need to build a baby's room. She hoped that
he'd answer his phone because she was leaving tomorrow
morning to go with Daniel to pick up Josiah's things, they
would be gone for a week. Luckily, he was in his shop.
She introduced herself and explained what she needed
and how she knew about him. *(I hope this won't take long, I*
still need to pack a few things to be ready to leave with Daniel
tomorrow morning, time is running out on me).

"Oh! My son called me last night and told me, I'd love
to help you out, that build-a-baby-room shower sounds
like a good idea," he said. "Would you mind if I used
that concept here? That would increase our business. Joe's
brother John is my partner now since Joe quit to become
a sheriff. My name is Carl by the way. Do you know what
type of wood they want?"

"Yes, they chose oak." (her favorite too)

"Okay the next question is do you want two of
everything?"

"Yes even the rocking chairs. That way they can both
rock a baby at the same time if needed. Plus the grandparents will be there for two months, and I can't see the grandmas not wanting to be up there too. Can you send all the
materials and the designs to my ranch? I'll need them by
the fifteenth. Or do you think sooner so that Joe can have
time to check it all out? Oh I also need materials to make
two rocking horses, they don't need to be in oak though."

"Don't you think they will be too young to ride for
awhile?" he asked.

"Yes but my foreman's son, who is five, wants to make them with his daddy." Charity's mind wanders off thinking about Daniel and Josiah

"Oh, I understand no problem."

"What tools will the men need to bring with them?" She then asked. *Her mind back on the task at hand*

"Just the things Joe recommended," Carl responded.

She then gave him her credit card number and her address and thanked him for everything. As she was putting her credit card back in her wallet, Carl ended the call with, "Don't you worry my Joe will see that it all gets done properly." They hung up after that. She then covered the dessert and headed upstairs to finish her packing for the trip.

On Saturday night, they had a traditional BBQ to culminate the guests' vacation. Simon did the cooking for everyone. Charity would always appear to thank them for coming and inviting them to return if they enjoyed it and to let their friends and neighbors know about them too. She was glad this was the last group for the year. She would be busy for the next month with the baby shower and loved it when she could just enjoy the property she had at a slower pace.

The Childs came up to her after the BBQ and joyfully exclaimed this was the *best* vacation they have ever had and not just because of Daniel and Josiah either.

"I understand that you're coming with Daniel to pick up Josiah's belongings. I want you to know that I am okay with your relationship with him," Vicki said. "I loved my daughter, but I know she didn't want to have this child, and she didn't love Daniel. I can see that you love him and that he loves you, and I want to wish you a happy future with him."

"Thank you, Mrs. Childs," Charity said softly. "But for the moment we are only friends. I don't know if he has said anything about where he works but he came here while I was in the hospital recovering from an accident and had just lost my family. I hated everyone and he refused to let me stay that way. I could see his despair also."

"Honey, it's much more than that but you two will just have to find that out for yourselves. Can we still see him?" Vicki replied.

"I don't have the authority to answer that Mrs. Childs but I would hope that Daniel would never break those ties," Charity responded. "I know that I wouldn't, my family meant everything to me before the accident. I miss them so much but it's getting easier for me to talk about them now."

"Daniel did tell us a little about your accident, which is why he was offered the job. I believe that God intends for you two to heal each other, and I'm seeing that already in him and it sounds as though you are healing also." Charity smiled but didn't say anything. "Let's just let God continue to do his work in both of you."

"Thank you, Mrs. Childs. I appreciate your comforting words."

At that moment, Daniel walked up with Josiah and said, "I was just talking to Josh and told him that Josiah could ride home with them since he has been with me for the past two weeks. They need their time with him too."

Josiah held out his arms to his grandma. "Can I have a hug, Grandma?"

"Of course you can, sweetheart. Come here."

Daniel handed him over to his grandma. "Josh and I were talking about leaving around nine o'clock tomorrow morning. Does that suit you two ladies?"

"Sounds good to me," Charity responded. "Why don't you and Josh come to the house and we can all have breakfast together before we head on out,"—she looked at Vicki—"say eight o'clock?"

"I'd love to. When we travel, Josh just stops at a fast food place, goes to the drive thru, and makes me eat while we drive."

"I forgot to mention at choir practice that we wouldn't be there tomorrow," Daniel asked Charity. "Did you mention it to anyone?"

She patted his hands. "Yes, I did. So don't worry."

Vicki noticed the intimate gesture, and she now knew what she needed to know about their relationship, whether they wanted to admit it or not. They said good night to each other and departed to their own rooms.

Vicki went to Josh and told him what she saw and what she Charity had talked about. Josh smiled and replied, "Maybe this was meant to be. God works in mysterious ways honey."

CHAPTER 19

Sunday morning at seven-thirty, Charity was in the kitchen making homemade cinnamon rolls and sandwiches and snacks for them to take on the road. She'd already packed her bag and had chopped up the ingredients for the omelets she would be making. At quarter to eight, Daniel and Josiah walked in and volunteered to help make breakfast.

Josiah smelled and asked, "What is that?"

"That my son is Charity's cinnamon rolls. You're going to love them."

"Can I help you with anything?" Daniel asked.

"Yes, you can set the table, I have everything else under control. Now excuse me I need to start the omelets."

She turned her back to him but looked back and winked. Daniel smiled and started to set the table.

At eight o'clock, the Childs knocked and Josiah went to let them in.

"Grandma, Miss Charity made cinnamon rolls!"

"Oh my, that does sound good sweetie," Vicki said. "Did you wash your hands?"

"Yes, Grandma. Daddy made me, come on I want one." He tugged his grandma to the table. Charity was just walking in with the omelets and hash browns, and Daniel was right behind her with the cinnamon rolls.

"Who's hungry?" he asked.

They all responded, "I am!"

Jess had walked in behind them, and he asked Josh to say grace. Then they all sat down to eat.

"Charity, all this looks so good!" Vicki said, and Josh agreed.

Vicki and Charity cleaned up as Daniel and Josh took the snacks and sandwiches out to the vehicles. Then Charity grabbed her bag, handed it to Daniel and said, "I'm ready to go, you all set?"

"Yes."

Vicki, Josh and Josiah were just getting in their car as they walked out to Daniel's truck. *Head 'em up and move 'em out*, she thought. As they made their way, Daniel kept the conversation on basics, but he kept looking at her and wishing she would slide over closer to him. She was thinking the same thing although she was too afraid to voice it aloud.

When it was time for lunch, Josh had actually pulled over to a diner.

"Thankfully Josiah had to use the bathroom, otherwise we would have had fast food on the road, again!" Vicki said.

Charity looked at Daniel after she had said that and agreed she had found out from previous conversations with him that he and Josh were similar in that manner.

At around six, they pulled into the motel parking lot they decided on staying during lunch. Josiah jumped out of the car and ran to Daniel.

"Guess what Dad? Grandpa said they have cowboy sheets on the beds here for kids, isn't that cool?"

Daniel picked him up. "Yes that is cool. Are you hungry?" he asked him.

"Oh yes! I told Grandma hours ago I was, but grandpa said I had to wait a little longer until we got here. Can we eat now?"

All the adults grinned and replied, "Yes"

While Josiah and the women went into the restaurant Daniel and Josh went into the motel office, registered, and got the room keys. They walked next door to the restaurant to have dinner. After they had ordered their food, Josh told them about the sleeping arrangements.

"You women will be in one room and the men will be in the room right next to you. I asked them to remember to use the cowboy's sheets for you Josiah."

"Cool Grandpa".

Their food came then so they ate until they were full and went to get the luggage from the cars after. Josiah knocked on the adjoining door saying, "Grandma, can I come in?"

"Yes, Sweetie. Just open the door."

He opened the door while saying, "Guess what? They have cowboys and Indians sheets!"

"I bet you'll have dreams of them while you are sleeping, since you didn't have a nap today. Are you getting tired?"

"No. Dad told he would take me to the playground for a little if I promised not to complain when it's time for a bath, and I said okay! Does that mean I am a big boy now?"

"Yes, honey that does," she said and hugged her grandson. "You're getting to be such a good little man. Grandma is going to miss you so much when you go back with Daddy and Miss Charity.". He grinned and said, "Dad told me that I'll get my own horse when we get back."

Charity leaned over. "I think you will be the best owner for Star. I am sure you'll treat her right."

"Star will be mine? Way cool!"

"Josiah," Vicki spoke up, "what did I teach you to say when somebody does something nice for you."

He piped up, "I'm supposed to say thank you." Turning towards Charity he said, "Thank you, Miss Charity. I'll take good care of Star, I'll feed her and bath her and ride her."

Charity squatted down and looked him in the eye. "You forgot the most important thing of all you have to love her."

Josiah beamed. "Oh that's so easy! I already do."

Daniel knocked on the door to interrupt them. "Are you ready to go to the playground now? Anyone else want to come along?"

Both women and Josiah answered, "Yes," each for their own reasons.

Vicki knew in her heart that Josiah should be with his daddy. As the time got closer for him to leave them though, she just needed to be around him for as long as possible.

Thankfully, Daniel had realized that and had let Josiah ride back with them this last time. *What am I going to do without my sweet little boy*, she thought. Josh came out to the playground for the same reason. Charity went out to the playground because she felt drawn to both Daniel and Josiah. Josiah, like any child went because he wanted to play.

After an hour of taking turns pushing the swing, they all went inside so that Josiah could get into his pajamas.

"Grandma, will you read me my favorite story?" he asked. Then he turned to his dad and asked, "Will you tuck me in first?"

"Can Grandpa do it tonight instead?" Daniel replied. "They love you so much but they are also going to miss you so much when you come to live with me. I would like you to be a good little man and allow them this trip back home to take care of you. Okay, son?"

"Okay, Daddy. I love them, too. Do you think they can come live with us one day? I think I would like that."

"Son, they are always welcome," he answered in a cracking voice with so much emotion.

After Vicki and Josh tucked him in and read to him, they all turned in themselves. Traveling was very tiring for everyone.

The next morning they packed up everything and had breakfast at the restaurant before leaving. By six o'clock in the evening, they should be home if all went smoothly. Unfortunately, things didn't go smoothly about an hour down the road the storm that was expected came blowing in fiercely. Quickly the visibility dissipated, the rear lights of the car ahead of them disappeared from sight. Daniel tried to stay close enough to keep them in sight. After fifteen minutes, he asked Charity to call them on their cell phone and ask if they knew of a safe place for them to pull over to wait out the storm. Vicki answered on the first ring.

"Charity, Josh says about two miles down the road, there should be a general store we can stop at."

Charity relayed the information to Daniel and he sighed. "That will be a big relief. My neck and shoulder muscles are tightening up already."

It turned out to be three miles, but the general store had installed bright fog lights on its building so that travelers could see it and stop. When they walked into the store they were greeted by the owner.

"Hello, strangers. I see you saw my lights from the road," he said. "We tend to have dense fog around here this time of year. My wife suggested I light this place up like a Christmas tree years ago because she got lost once and couldn't find her way back home."

"Yes, we did and please thank her for us." Charity remarked as she extended her hand in greeting.

"My dear wife departed five years ago, but many a traveler has been thankful for those lights, me too actually, this way I get to have visitors. Would you all like a cup of coffee? Well, maybe some hot chocolate instead for the boy."

"Oh, yes please, that sounds great." Vicki added to the conversation.

He led them into another room where he had placed a few tables and chairs around. The next hour, a few more travelers had found him and the place was soon full. Henry, the owner, loved to talk and told stories about what it was like when he first moved here and built his place.

As noon time approached Henry told everyone not to worry he would light up the grill and make some grub for them all. Josiah walked up to him and yanked on his shirt to get his attention.

"Sir, can you just make me a hot dog. I don't think I like grub, and it doesn't sound very good either."

As everyone laughed and got a kick out of the little boy, Daniel quickly walked up to him and picked him up. "Son, grub just means food. It isn't polite to be picky."

"Oh you mean like cowboy food, Dad?"

"Yes son, like cowboy food."

Josiah turned to Henry and asked, "Are you a cowboy?"

"No, sir. I was a prospector."

"What's that," he asked.

"Well sonny, that means I dug for gold."

"You did?" he asked with his eyes wide open. "That sounds like fun."

"No it was hard work, but I found enough to buy this land and build this store and my home. Alicia, my wife, told me she wouldn't marry me until I had a house and a job. I loved her so much that very day I quit and built her a house." He smiled to himself as the memories flooded him. "Would you like anything else besides a hot dog, young man?"

"Do you have any macaroni and cheese? That is my favorite."

"Yes I do. I'll make some right now, enough for everyone."

"Thank you, mister." Daniel just shrugged his shoulders and walked away. What else could he do? Henry made enough food for everyone and extra in case another group of strangers showed up.

Around two, the storm finally decreased enough so that the visibility was better and they could travel again. They all thanked Henry for the food and the stories to entertain them. As Josiah was walking out the door, he turned back and hollered out.

"Mr. Henry? I'm sure glad you were here. Thank you for the grub and I like stories." Henry grinned. "Come back by here anytime son."

The adults had decided they would still drive straight through; Josiah could sleep in the car. If all things went smoothly, this time they would arrive around midnight.

Thankfully, the rest of the trip went smoothly. They rolled into The Childs' driveway a little before midnight. Josh carried Josiah into his bedroom and Vicki tucked him in and then went to make up the guest bedrooms for Charity and Daniel.

When Josiah woke up in the morning, he came running into the kitchen asking where his daddy was. Charity and Vicki were making breakfast.

"Your daddy is still asleep as far as I know," Charity told Josiah. "Why don't you go find him and tell him it's time to get up. Breakfast will be ready in a few minutes."

Charity turned back to the stove as she commented, "That boy sure has a lot of energy, how do you keep up with him?"

Vicki sighed deeply. "I usually don't and that is one reason we're glad Daniel is ready to take over. We just aren't as young as we used to be."

Charity laughed. "Good to know, thanks for the warning. I will be taking care of him during the day after school and Daniel will have the evening and night shifts. With my leg, I hope I won't have any trouble."

"Just tell him to slow down."

"My mom used to tell me that all the time."

Since Daniel had bought him all new furniture, all they had to pack up was Josiah's clothes. As they were packing it, Josiah had to tell them which was new for school and which were his play clothes and such. He was so excited he couldn't stop talking. Charity thought, *either Daniel hasn't been excited about anything or Josiah took after his mother because Daniel had never talked as much as Josiah had this morning.*

They were all packed and ready to head back after lunch. Vicki and Josh gave Josiah several hugs and kisses before they could let him go. They promised to come see him at Thanksgiving and Christmas since they had discussed it during breakfast.

Charity gave them both hugs and whispered into Vicki's ear, "Keep me in your prayers. I will definitely need strength to keep up with him."

Vicki smiled and answered back, "I don't think you will have any problems, but we will keep all three of you in our prayers."

They drove until dinnertime and found a motel to stay at for the evening.

"Can we stop tomorrow and say hi to Mr. Henry?" Josiah asked his daddy.

"Yes, son. I think we can do that."

"Thank you, Daddy," he said and hugged his dad.

The next day they were coming up to Henry's place around noon. Josiah had been looking out the window for it.

"There it is Daddy!" he exclaimed when he saw it. "On the left, you said we could stop and I am hungry."

When they parked, he jumped out and went running up the steps.

"Mr. Henry! I came back to see you just like I said."

Henry came around from the counter. "So you did, son. Where are you going now?"

"Back home to live with my daddy now, before we were going to get my clothes from Grandma and Grandpa's house. Daddy lives on a ranch and he's teaching me how to ride a horse and I even get one of my own. Miss Charity said I have to love it and bath it and feed it, her name is Star because of the one on her head."

"That's a lot of words out of a little boy," Henry told him.

"I talk all the time," Josiah told him. "I just have so many things to say, just like you Mr. Henry!"

Henry laughed. "So you do young man, so you do."

"I'm hungry. Do you have any food I can have?"

Daniel walked up to him then and said, "Josiah, we talked about this on the way here. We are going to buy some things from his store and we will make sandwiches but we can eat them here if Mr. Henry will open up the other room."

"Okay, Dad. I forgot, sorry," Josiah mumbled.

"Yes I'll open the other room and turn on the grill so you can make hot sandwiches," Henry said. "A grilled cheese sounds good to me right now."

"Me too! Can we, Daddy?"

"Yes, it sounds good to me," Daniel said. "Thank you, Henry."

As they were leaving, Henry grabbed a red bandana off his shelves and handed it to Josiah. "Here, son. Every cowboy needs one of these. Do you know how to wear it?"

"No, sir, I don't. Will you do it? That is, if my dad will let me have it. I'm not supposed to ask for things."

Henry kneeled down to put it on him. "Your daddy gives you good advise Josiah. Always listen to him."

"Yes sir, Mr. Henry, I will and have a good day!"

At lunch, Charity and Daniel had agreed to drive straight through. They both felt as if they needed to be back home as soon as possible for some reason.

CHAPTER 20

An hour later, Jess called and told her that he was at the emergency room; they were checking out Simon who had burned himself badly. They said something about second-degree burns. He spilled a pan of hot grease and tried to catch it but it went all over his hands and down his legs.

"Why he tried to catch it I have no idea, he should've known better," Jess said.

"We're on our way but we're still about eight hours away," Charity said. "I'll call the house right now and tell the men to pray for Simon and to elect someone to cook for today. I can take over tomorrow morning."

They rolled into the yard just after ten o'clock in the evening. Jess came walking out of the bunkhouse because he had heard them.

"They're keeping Simon overnight for observation but they say he should be able to come home tomorrow after the doc checks him out. They bandaged up both his hands and just salved his legs. If he hadn't tried to catch that darn pan he wouldn't have both his hands bandaged up the doctor told me."

"Thanks Jess I'll go to the hospital tomorrow morning after I make breakfast and get things together for a cold lunch," Charity said. "Daniel and Josiah will be busy getting Josiah's things put away, would you care to ride along with me?"

"Yes Charity, I would like to ride along with you. Simon is my best friend after all."

"Okay then, Jess, But right now, I'm tired so I will say good night," she said with a yawn. "See you in the morning, and please be sure to let the men know breakfast will be here at the house."

In the morning Charity was making breakfast, slicing up meats for the men's lunch, had potatoes and eggs boiling for a potato salad. As the men came in, she served them scrambled eggs and country potatoes along with fresh OJ and warmed tortillas. She then went back into the kitchen to finish making the potato salad. She added a bowl of baked beans to go along with everything, sliced up some sourdough bread and some marbled rye.

That should be enough, she thought. *The men can get their own condiments.*

Daniel announced that Miss Charity and Jess were heading into town to get Simon and he would be in the stable putting Josiah's things away if they needed anything. They were all told their assignments the night before by Jess.

Jess and Charity drove into town to the hospital around nine o'clock.. They found out that the doctor was with Simon right then. The nurse told them to go have a seat in the waiting room and she would call when they could go in. About half an hour later she said it will be another thirty minutes because they were still writing up his discharge papers.

She gave them instructions as to what he could and couldn't do. By the time she was through, another nurse was wheeling him into the lobby. Simon spotted them.

"Am I ever glad to see you two," he said. "I feel like an old fool."

"And you look like one too," Jess answered back.

Charity swatted him on the arm. "Jess that is not nice to say to him. I'm sure he's in a lot of pain."

"I would be except they gave me painkillers ten minutes ago," Simon answered. "Now, can we get home?"

"Glad to. I'll just go get the truck and pull up to the entrance and then we will be on our way," Charity replied.

"Hey Charity, why not kill two birds with one stone, get your cast cut off!" Jess said. "Very funny, Jess. It isn't a cast it's a brace and I don't need a doctor to take it off, the doctor will tell me when the time is right. Besides, I don't even notice it anymore."

Simon just laughed at the two. "Come on, guys. Let's just go home, I don't want the pain to start again before we get home."

Daniel and Josiah were waiting at the bunkhouse door for them as they drove up. Jess got out of the back door as Daniel had just reached the front door to open it for Simon.

Simon looked at him. "Don't you start on me too, Jess has already said I look like a fool this morning."

Daniel looked over to Jess in disbelief.

"Hey he started it," Jess said in defense. "He said he felt like a fool and I just couldn't resist."

Daniel tried not to laugh thinking good thing those two are best friends.

Charity waited for them to get Simon out and then leaned out the window. "Are you sure you don't want to stay with me up at the house?"

"Now why would I do that missy," Simon said. "All the guys are out here, I won't be embarrassed by them when I need help getting dressed."

"Oh, sorry Simon, I wasn't thinking about that," Charity muttered.

The men got Simon all settled in while Charity parked the truck and walked up to the house.

I need to get dinner started, but I don't have enough supplies, she thought. *I need to check the bunkhouse kitchen to see what supplies they have.*

She walked back to the bunkhouse kitchen and started looking around. Thankfully, Simon has just restocked everything. She took out a few chickens to make fried chicken and dumplings. She then walked into the bunkhouse to announce that she would be cooking from the bunkhouse kitchen until she could go to the market and restock her supplies.

"Can I get some lunch?" Simon asked. "I'm starving."

"Do you want what the men had?" Charity asked him. "I made cold cuts and potato salad."

"Sounds good to me but whose is going to feed me?"

It was Jess who responded. "Your best friend of course. In fact I'll join you since I missed lunch too."

"You old coot," Simon teased, "you would eat anytime of the day or night, whether you had just ate or not."

"You better watch it you old fool, I won't feed you!" Jess warned, and they both laughed because they knew that wouldn't happen.

Charity put the chickens on to boil and then walked up to the house to grab her laptop. *Might as well work on the bookwork while I am at it.* She returned to the bunkhouse, "Jess where are the receipts from last week?" "I left them on Daniel's desk in the stable office."

"Thanks Jess" Charity called Daniel on his cell, "Can you grab the receipts off your desk and bring them to me at the bunkhouse please, I'd really appreciate it." A few minutes later, Josiah came running in.

"Daddy is on his way, can I help Simon and Jess?"

Charity smiled. "You need to ask them Josiah, not me."

He turned to Simon. "Simon, can I help you?"

"Sure! Jess wants to play checkers, so if I tell you what to move, can you do it?"

"Yes, I think I can."

Simon winked at him. "Well then sit down and help me beat Jess."

"Okay!" the energetic kid said. They kept Josiah busy for the next couple of hours. Daniel was out checking on things with the men, and Charity watched them from the table doing her books.

This is nice, she thought, *so this is the way it's going to be with Josiah living here.*

Just then, she realized that school would be starting in a few days. *Oh my…am I ready for this?*

Daniel came in to check on Josiah two hours later. He sat down next to Charity, "Do you realize that school starts in three days? With everything that has been going on I had forgotten about it."

Charity smiled. "Me too, but I think everything will turn out okay, even with Simon's injury."

"Do you know that this is the first time since the accident that September 1 came and went and I didn't even remember it?" Nobody spoke for a moment, and Charity broke the silence. "I enjoyed traveling with you so much that I forgot. Thank you, Daniel. You are truly helping me to heal."

"Well…" Charity paused then continued on.

"It's time I earn my keep and get back to cooking, the men should be returning soon." She walked away and Daniel just stared at her pondering on her comment.

Dinner was ready just in time the men had all returned and were ready and waiting. Jess asked Todd to say the Grace. Charity had made up a couple of pans of lasagna for Sunday's meal while making tonight's dinner. Simon asked to ride along with Charity in the morning, as he wanted to talk to Mrs. Davis.

Mrs. Davis was out on the lawn when Simon and Charity drove up. She came over as quickly as she could, opened his door and asked after him. Simon grimaced a little, "I'm fine but could we speak alone for a few minutes?"

"Virginia, I was wondering if you could spare some time to come out to the ranch this week and bring a few casseroles. Charity is going to have her hands full with school starting, the shopping, doing the books, her committees, and planning Amy's baby shower. She doesn't realize it but it's going to take some time to adjust to the new schedule."

"Of course, Simon I'll speak to a few of the ladies today and don't you worry, I'll deliver them personally tomorrow."

"Thanks, Virginia. I was hoping I could count on you, please don't let her know though okay?"

"You can count on me Simon."

Before Charity realized it, Sunday had flown by. *Tomorrow school starts*, she thought. *How am I going to juggle everything?* She then started making out a schedule.

"Okay, breakfast first, do my bookwork, make and serve lunch, start dinner, by then I'll need to go pick up Josiah, then I'll head over to the market that should get us home in time for me to finish dinner," she said to herself while jotting down her schedule.

On Monday afternoon when she got back from town, she saw Mrs. Davis' car parked near the bunkhouse. She called Daniel on his cell to let him know they were home and started unloading the groceries. Josiah helped her as he was still telling her every minute of his day. She smiled and thought, *this kid sure loves to talk!*

Daniel walked in just as he was through telling Charity about his day, but he started all over again to tell his dad. At that point, she smiled and excused herself to go see to dinner, as she walked toward the bunkhouse, she noticed that Mrs. Davis' car was gone.

Simon greeted her as she walked in. "Guess what Mrs. Davis brought by? The ladies in the church got together and made up some casserole dishes, saying they wanted to help out since I couldn't cook right now."

"Simon..." Charity cried. "Did you ask them to do this? Is this why you wanted to talk to her yesterday? Don't you think I can do it?"

"No, Charity. She called when she heard I was home but wouldn't believe I was okay until she saw me. That's why I wanted to talk to her you know how Virginia can get. Besides, you know how the ladies in the church are. If anyone is sick they make enough food to feed an army."

"Okay, Simon. I believe you just for that reason alone."

After she left, Simon sent up a silent prayer asking for forgiveness for the lie he had just told to her.

Charity then walked back to the house, Josiah was just finishing telling his dad all about his first day at school. She smiled because of the look of bewilderment on Daniel's face.

"Can I go out and see Star now?" Josiah asked. "I need to tell her all about my day too." Daniel gave Charity a what-have-I-got-myself-into look then turned to his son. "Yes, I'll be there in just a minute, be careful now."

"Don't forget to grab an apple for her, Josiah," Charity hollered out.

He grinned. "Can I share some of it with Sarah too?"

"Alright, but maybe you should wait to cut it until your Dad gets there."

"Okay!" he exclaimed as he was running out the door.

Charity smiled and told Daniel, "He reminds me of myself when I was younger. I ran all the time to, I was just so excited about life."

Daniel walked up to her and ran his finger down her cheek. "I wish I could have seen that."

Charity blushed as he did that and yet leaned into it wanting more. Daniel however stopped and sighed.

"I'd better get out there so he doesn't start without me. I never realized just how much energy he had before his coming here."

Charity laughed. "Maybe he'll slow down in another forty years or so."

"That's what I'm afraid of," Daniel groaned and walked out the door. He could hear her laughing as he closed the door.

Daniel rushed out to the stables, and Josiah met him at the door.

"I was just coming to get you, Dad."

"I'm here now, so let me cut the apple." Josiah ran to the stalls and fed Sarah first.

"You're the mom so you go first," he crooned. "I'll feed Star hers after."

Daniel was glad that Josiah was here, he wondered why he had waited so long. It just felt right being in his life every day. He sent up a prayer for Josh and Vicki, thankful they had forced the issue on him and hoping they were coping well with the change.

Charity was thankful the ladies had made so much food it made things easier for her during that first week. Doc Jensen came out Wednesday to check Simon's hands and changed his bandages.

"One more week and your brace and his bandages can come off," he told Charity. "Call my office and get an appointment for both of you. Oh by the way, my wife told me if you need any more food to just let her or Virginia know. They would be glad to send more out, anything for Simon."

"Wait Doc, what are you talking about?"

"Just that Simon had asked them to make some food to help you out."

Charity smiled sweetly. "You tell your wife thank you for me then, will you?" Then she turned to Simon and stared him down. "You lied to me Simon."

Doc looked at both of them and asked, "What's going on here?"

"Nothing much Doc," Charity responded. "It's just that I point-blank asked Simon if he had asked for food because he didn't think I could handle it and he told me no."

Doc grimaced. "I didn't know. I wouldn't have said anything."

"No I'm glad you did because now I know the truth," she took a deep breath, "excuse me please." She then walked out the door.

Doc looked at Simon. "I'm truly sorry, I didn't know."

Simon sighed as he got up to follow Charity. "I was just trying to help her."

Simon went after her and found her in Sarah's stall crying.

"Charity, please forgive me," Simon pleaded. "I just wanted to make things easier for you. This was your first week having to take care of Josiah, me and everything else."

Charity was sobbing. "I know, and I forgive you. I was going to tell you this morning that I was actually glad that they had brought it, but I chickened out and then Doc showed up," she said in between sobs. "Thank you for thinking of me Simon."

"Honey, I just wanted things to go smoothly for you," he touched her head and tried to calm her down. "Taking on the responsibilities for a small child is a huge thing, and you already do so much around here and then I did this and made more work for you."

She stood up, and they hugged. They both walked back to the bunkhouse.

CHAPTER 21

Daniel had been in the office and had overheard the whole conversation; he had been tempted to go out to comfort her when he first heard her crying but wanted to give her a moment alone. He was glad he had after Simon had walked in. He wondered if he was expecting too much of her to help him out. He decided he needed to call Vicki and see what she thought. Vicki answered on the first ring.

"Hi, Daniel! Is everything okay?"

"Do you have a minute, Vicki? I'd like to talk if you do."

"Sure, Daniel. What about"

"Charity," he replied, "Do you think I am asking too much of her to watch Josiah? I just overheard something between Simon and her that got me wondering. You see, Simon burned his hands before we got back—second-degree burns—and can't do anything and with taking on Josiah do you think it is too much on her?"

"Daniel, Charity has many responsibilities running that ranch but no. I don't think it's too much to ask of her. It may take her a week or so to get things all figured out, but I'm sure that she'll have no problems, especially with Simon needing care but things will work out. Just give it time."

"Thanks, Vicki. I'm glad we're still close, with my folks dead, I think of you as my mom."

"Daniel, that means so much to me to hear that. Thank you, we love you too."

Daniel hung up and tried to think about how he could help Charity adjust. He decided to go talk to Jess. He walked over to the bunkhouse, and Charity passed him going out as he walked in.

"I'm heading into town do you need anything?" she said.

"Actually if you could wait a minute, I would like to go with you."

She seemed surprised by that comment but shrugged and went on. "Okay it should be about five to ten minutes before I'll be ready, but you can come along if you wish."

"That should give me enough time to do what I needed here," Daniel responded. "Meet you at the truck, yours or mine?"

Charity grinned. "Mine, I'm in the mood to drive."

Daniel went over to Jess and Simon and asked, "How can I make this adjusting time any better for Charity?"

"Let us think on it," Simon said.

"Yes," Jess agreed. "Simon tried something last Sunday and it seems to have backfired on him. It really hurt her feelings."

Daniel grimaced. "I know, I overhead them just now in the stable talking. I feel so bad, like it's my fault."

Simon piped up. "You? I'm the one who burned my hands so she had to take on even more responsibilities around here. You go into town with her and Jess and I will try to come up with something and let you know."

"Okay, I think I'd better go then," Daniel said.

Daniel felt weird about Charity driving, but he didn't let her know. He tried to keep the conversation going but Charity didn't seem in the mood to talk.

"Charity," he finally said, "we need to talk about Josiah and what I had asked you to do for me."

She glanced over and he thought he saw hurt in her eyes. "Why Daniel?" she cried. "Don't you think I can handle it either?"

"Of course I think you can handle it, otherwise I wouldn't have asked. But now with Simon, it may be too much on you."

"Oh, Daniel! It isn't that at all, I'm just feeling over-whelmed, I just never thought about how my mom coped with all the responsibilities and yet she did it. I just need to get some confidence and figure out the best way to do things. This is nothing new to a rancher, but I never had to do it. My folks always handled everything, I am just missing my mom."

"I know how you feel," Daniel told her. "When Josiah was born, I didn't know what to do and my folks were already dead so I turned to Vicki. I even called her before I came to the bunkhouse. I asked her if she thought I'd asked too much of you, I told her about Simon too." "Really, Daniel?"

"Yes really, and do you want to hear her response?"

"Yes."

"She said she thinks you are a wonderful person to just give you time to adjust to all these changes but that she feels you can do it."

"That does make me feel so much better hearing that. Thank you."

"So, how can I help you to adjust?"

"Well…" she paused, "once my brace comes off next week it won't be as hard. Besides, I will have had two weeks practice already by then. I wonder if all new mother's feel this way?" "Now that I can't tell you Charity, but I'm sure you have some friends that could answer that question. However, I've already said I trust you with Josiah so that doesn't come into it does it?"

"No, it's just the timing of everything I am worried about. Daniel, just knowing that you support me in this is enough for me. Thank you."

"Charity, I hope you know that you have become a big part of my life. I truly wish for us to go even further in our relationship. I promise I'll never do to you what Jimmy did."

"I know that, Daniel, and I would like to further our relationship also," she shyly replied.

"Well…"

"We have arrived, do you want to go in and get Josiah or shall we both go?"

"Let's both go," he stated.

When Josiah saw his dad and Charity, he ran to them and hugged them both.

"Guess what we did today, we got to play with a baby goat!" Charlie brought it in for show and tell.

"You didn't tell me it was show and tell day, Josiah," Daniel replied.

"That's because I didn't have anything to show, Dad."

Charity smiled at the simple logic of the boy. Sophia walked in then to pick up Matthew and waved to Charity and Daniel.

"That's Matthew's mommy," Josiah said. "He said once his sister is born then he's going to bring her in for show and tell day."

Charity tried to explain to Josiah that may not be possible but just then Sophia walked over and Josiah spoke up "Hello, Matthew's mommy! Are you going to let Matthew bring in his sister for show and tell day after she is born? He said he was going to bring her."

Sophia smiled. "I don't know, he hasn't even asked me yet."

Charity and Daniel smirked and thought that was a good answer.

CHAPTER 22

Josiah was waving to all his new friends as they drove away, then turned to his Dad

"Can I have a party with all my new friends? I like this school."

Daniel looked over at Charity and she shrugged. "Josiah we're already planning a party for Miss Amy in a few weeks and they can come then okay?"

"Cool then I can show them the horse my dad and I made for her babies."

That got Charity's wheels thinking. *Maybe I could find a project that the kids could make. I need to call Joe and see what he thinks and then call Cindy.*

She asked Daniel to drive them home, so she could make some phone calls. First, she called the Sheriff's office but Joe wasn't in so she called his dad. Carl answered and she explained what she was thinking.

"Would you trust them with paint? John made some wooden blocks while practicing on the new lathe so I could send those to you. There are a couple of sets. Would that be enough, one has animals and the other has letters. I can get him to make up a set of numbers if you want?"

"That sounds great if he has the time. Just let me know! Now I need to call Cindy and change the wording on the invitations. Have a nice day Mr. Casey and thank you for the wonderful idea, good-bye."

"Daniel, can we turn around and go see Cindy or do we need to get straight home?" Charity asked.

Daniel turned the truck around "This is your day, Charity. Your chariot is yours to command."

So they headed back to the store and Charity hopped out and let the men come in after her. She found Cindy at the checkout stand but had no customer's right then. *Perfect*, she thought, and then proceeded to tell her the newest idea.

"That should be fun!" Cindy exclaimed. "The invitations will get here tomorrow and I have Friday off. Can we do them then?"

Charity nodded. "What time, my place or yours?" Just then Charity's cell phone rang it was Joe calling her back. She told him what she had done

"This is going to be some baby shower," Joe said. "I am really looking forward to it, if you need anything else just let me know."

"Your house at ten?" Cindy asked when Charity hung up.

"Sounds good to me, Cindy. See you Friday morning."

Daniel and Josiah had opted to stay in the truck, so she rushed back out and giggled. "Homeward please, Mr. Chariot driver."

"Your wish is my command, my lady!"

Once they got home, Charity went to warm up the casserole she had gotten out for dinner. Then she remembered she needed to call the doctor's office to set up the appointment for both her and Simon, so she quickly dialed Doc's office. She made the appointment for next Wednesday. When it was dinnertime, she served the men and took over feeding Simon, that's when she told him his appointment was for one-thirty in the afternoon. Afterwards they would pick Josiah up from school. She then realized that she wasn't stressing as much about coping with everything.

The next morning as Daniel drove Josiah to school. Charity was in the bunkhouse trying to get a volunteer to oversee the kids and assist painting the blocks during the shower. Todd volunteered to do it because that way he doesn't have to assist Simon with the cooking. Charity then had to get a volunteer to help Simon with the cooking—Randy volunteered for that job.

Now I need volunteers to help set up everything. Every man there agreed to assist with setting things up. Charity thanked all of them and left to call Mr. Casey to ask when the rocking chair materials would arrive since this new development. She knew Josiah would want to paint blocks too with his friends.

John answered the phone this time. "Oh, Ms. Stewart. No my father isn't here right now, how can I help you?"

"I had ordered materials to make rocking horses and now that the children will be painting your blocks, I'll need to get the rocking horse materials ASAP. Josiah wants to show all his friends what he and his dad built."

"Sure, Ms. Stewart. I'll get those sent to you immediately. Two horses, correct?"

"Yes two as they are having twins. Is there any possibility that either or both of you would like to come to the shower? I'll put you up here, that way you could have a good visit with Joe."

"Thank you for the invitation. I'll ask him what he thinks when Dad gets back."

"I have enough rooms so that your mother could come also. I don't want her to be left out. Well thank you again John, good-bye."

Two hours later the phone rang and she answered it.

"Paradise Ranch, how may I help you?"

It was Joe. "Charity I don't know what it is about you but I just got a call from my folks and they said to tell you they would love to come. John too but it's not necessary for you to put them up, I have enough room at my place. I want you to know this is the first time they will have come to visit. Thank you. I've been trying to get them all to come but to no avail. My dad wants to meet you in person. My mom is thrilled, because Dad almost never closes the shop and goes anywhere."

"Oh Joe, I'm so happy for you then. Are you sure you have enough room?"

"Yes, I'm sure I bought the old Franklin house in town. You know, the two-story colonial. I had to do a lot of renovating to get it back to its former glory, but I'm done now and have repeatedly asked them to come and at least see the house but I could never get them out here."

Charity felt her heart burst out into signing, she was so happy. *Thank you, Lord for changing my life,* she thought.

Daniel was losing the battle against Charity, he wanted to be around her more and more. Each time he saw her now it was as if he was starving and needed her for his nourishment. He knew that he needed to up his game and make a commitment but was afraid. If only he knew Charity was thinking the same thing. She felt drawn to him as with a lasso. All she wanted was to call him *her* Daniel in real life.

Daniel arrived early for dinner, he came over to her and leaned against the counter. He really wanted to was kiss her, but he simply raised his hand and lovingly stroked her cheek. "Charity, will you go out with me on a real date?"

She paused in her preparations for dinner, reached over to put her hand on his. "Yes Daniel, I would like that very much."

"Okay then I made arrangements with Jess to babysit Josiah tomorrow night, so we can go out to dinner."

"Tomorrow night?"

"Yes, so wear your best dress because I made reservations at seven o'clock at a restaurant."

He couldn't help it—he just pulled her to him and gently kissed her cheek where he had stroked it. She leaned into him and placed her hand on his heart.

"Oh, Daniel! You do such wondrous things to my heart. I feel so loved when I am near you."

"That's what I want to talk about tomorrow night."

"Okay then, what time will we need to leave?" she asked.

"No later than quarter to six."

"I'll be ready and waiting for you. Now if you will excuse me I need to finish dinner preparations, please move aside. I don't think properly when you are so close."

"Me too," he whispered into her ear and walked away as requested.

I have an actual date with Daniel, she thought. She almost burned the rolls because of her daydreaming about him.

That evening during dinner, they kept sending each other looks and she blushed a lot. Jess took notice of it all and smiled, *finally they're beginning to respond to one another.*

Saturday afternoon Charity planned the Sunday meal. She didn't want anything to interfere with getting ready for her date, but she didn't want to forget about the men either. She made macaroni and cheese with dogs for Jess and Josiah's dinner. She went upstairs after that and took a bubble bath and got ready for her date. She felt as if she were sixteen again; she was so excited to spend time with Daniel.

At quarter to six on the dot, her doorbell rang. Daniel was standing there with a bouquet of flowers in his hand.

"How sweet of you, Daniel!" she said and put them in a vase and out the door they went.

When he opened her door, he asked her to scoot over to the middle because he wanted her next to him. At the restaurant, they sat in the lounge where a band was playing. They placed their order and then he asked her to dance. They fit well together, and she matched his steps to the music. To Charity, it was a romantic evening. Charity about cried, she was so thrilled. When he was through speaking, she took his hands in hers.

"I feel the same way about you. I never want it to end."

"Charity, will you marry me?" he asked.

"I know that we haven't dated but we have spent a lot of time together and been through so many things already. From the moment I saw you, I was yours. Please say yes and make me the happiest man alive." He pulled out a ring box and held it out to her. In it was a diamond and sapphire ring that looked like an antique. "Oh, Daniel! It's beautiful, yes I'll marry you! I couldn't live without you either."

Then they got up and danced some more. Holding each other was the perfect way to end the evening.

CHAPTER 23

The next morning upon waking, Charity looked down at her hand. It was real, Daniel proposed to her. She only wished that her folks were alive to see it, but she knew in her heart that they were smiling down on her from heaven.

Charity made breakfast for the ranch hands that morning. When she was serving, they all noticed the ring but they were waiting for someone else to say it first. When everyone sat, Daniel stood up to make the announcement, Jess and Simon both agreed that it was about time and all the men congratulated them.

After church was over, Charity rushed over to Amy and showed her the ring. Amy was so happy for her.

"Charity, you deserve happiness," Amy said and hugged her. "To think it took an accident to get you two together, just like Bruce and I. Thankfully we both recognized that fact and said yes. Have you set a date?"

"No," Charity replied, "I need time to get used to the idea first."

Daniel walked up to her after checking Josiah out of Sunday school and refused to leave her side.

Mr. Casey called the house around two in the afternoon.

"John had told us about the invitation to the baby shower and wanted to personally RSVP, but we are going to stay at Joe's. In fact we are coming a few days early! My wife is so happy that I'm closing the shop and taking a vacation. She wants to spend a few days at Joe's first. He has sent us pictures of the renovations but pictures are never as good as the real thing. So all your materials will be hand delivered by us. John is sending off the materials for the rocking horses tomorrow, they should be there by Wednesday."

"Oh Mr. Casey that sounds wonderful! I hope you all enjoy your vacation then," Charity replied.

"I told you my name is Carl and my wife's name is Susanna."

"Yes, Sir!" Charity grinned as she hung up the phone.

Tuesday afternoon after picking up Josiah from school, they headed over to the church for her Prison Ministries Committee meeting. Josiah played with Pastor Mark's grandchildren who were visiting.

"How long are they here for?" Charity asked the Pastor. "Will they still be here a week from this coming Saturday? They can come to the shower also! I'm sure the kids would have a fun time and your daughter and son-in law will too since they know so many of the families in town."

"Well they were actually leaving that day, but I will ask if they want to extend their stay another day because you invited them. I will call you and let you know."

After the meeting, they drove home so Josiah could finish his homework before dinner. Today he was supposed to draw a picture of his home. As he drew and colored on the kitchen table, Charity prepared the meal. When he was done, they walked down to the bunkhouse to remind Simon that they had a doctor's appointment the next day and to stop in the stable and give Sarah and Star a treat. Josiah went running into the stall and started chatting away to Star. Sarah nickered at him from her stall, too.

Daniel walked in from outside just as Charity was telling Josiah that his daddy should be coming in soon.

"I'm here," he spoke loudly, and Josiah jumped up and ran into his arms. "I missed you today, Daddy. What did you do? I played with Jeremiah and James during the meeting. They are visiting their Grandpa Mark."

"Well son how nice. What did you play?"

"Builders, I was telling them about the horses we are going to make. They want to come see them, then I told them about us getting to paint blocks for Miss Amy's new babies. They thought that was cool. I told them to come. Is that okay, Dad?" Then he took a deep breath!

Daniel ruffled his head "Well son, that should be fine but we will need to talk to their mom and dad to see if that is okay. Remember we always need to ask an adult first."

"I'm sorry, Daddy. I forgot."

"I know, son. It's hard to remember all the rules at once, but one day it won't be."

Charity had walked over to them and nodded. "I spoke with Pastor Mark and asked if they would still be here and invited them. He said he'd call me back after he spoke with his daughter and son in-law."

"Oh and Daniel don't forget tomorrow the materials for the horses will be delivered but Simon and I both have doctor's appointments tomorrow after we pick up Josiah, so please make sure someone keeps an eye out for them okay?"

"No problem, is your appointment tomorrow to affirm you can ditch the brace?" Daniel asked her "Yes and I will be so glad to finally have it off."

The next day, Pastor Mark called, "Charity my wife talked our daughter into staying for the party, so you can tell Josiah that Jeremiah and James will be coming to his party afterall." "Thanks Pastor Mark, he was kind of bummed that they couldn't make it, I'm sure this will cheer him up."

Yes no more brace, I hope they haven't called Simon's name yet.

As she walked into the waiting room they called Simon's name *(perfect timing she thought)* so she stayed to keep Josiah entertained, although the doctor's office seemed to have a variety of things to occupy children.

Simon came back out and only had a small bandage on one hand and grinning broadly. "Okay let's get home, I feel like cooking again."

"Are you insinuating that you have a problem with my cooking, Simon?"

"No ma'am, I just feel the need to cook."

"I know just how that feels." She smiled as Josiah looked up seriously.

"Will you teach me how to cook Simon," Josiah asked. "I want to feed my men when I get a ranch too."

Simon chuckled. "I'm sure we have lots of time before that happens, young man."

Daniel was waiting for them at the house.

"The materials just arrived with a note from Carl. He said if we have any problems just call Joe but they will be here next Wednesday with all the other materials."

They all checked it out and Charity asked Daniel, "Can you take Friday afternoon off? There's no school because of a field trip then you and Josiah can start making the rocking horses, do you think I can help too?"

"I'd love to spend time with my two favorite people. I'm sure Jess won't mind handling things for an afternoon, not that there's anything that really needs to be done."

Friday afternoon the trio assembled the rocking horses but they didn't varnish them as planned. Daniel squatted to be at Josiah's eye level, "Hey buddy, do you think that you and your friends would like to paint these guys the day of the party?" Josiah's eyes got as round as saucers, "Really Dad, you would let us do that? That would be way cool." "Of course son, I think you and your friends will do a wonderful job of painting." Then he stood up and Charity nodded her agreement that he had done the right thing.

One more week and this barn is going to be filled to the brim with a whole lot of people and furniture.

That evening Vicki and Josh called. "We got our invitation and we want to come," Vicki said. "Is there room at the house or should we get a hotel room?"

"The Casey's are staying at Joe's so we have plenty of room," Charity answered. "I'm so glad you decided to come back for this. It's going to be the party of the year it seems. I just hope Amy likes everything. I would be a wreck right now, only a month away and no nursery, but then she is so much more laid back then I will ever be."

Wednesday afternoon her phone rang. "Charity, my folks would like to meet you. Can we come over right now?"

"Yes, Joe. That's no problem I'm anxious to meet them too."

Forty minutes later, a truck and trailer arrived along with Joe's SUV. Everyone got out and Joe introduced his family to Daniel and Charity. Then they headed to the barn to store the materials for Saturday's party. Daniel grabbed a couple of men from the bunkhouse to help with the unloading. Then they all wanted a tour.

Susanna was amazed with the bunkhouse kitchen.

"This is bigger than mine!" she exclaimed. Simon strutted like a peacock showing his kitchen off. During the tour, Simon invited everyone to stay for dinner.

"That way the men could start setting things up for the party Saturday ahead of time."

The men all nodded and left to go out to the barn. Susanna opted to stay with Simon and Charity, so they put her to work also. Simon asked Charity to make a few pies so they would have enough dessert.

Simon leaned over to Susanna and said, "She makes the flakiest crusts I have ever tasted, except for her mother's."

A couple of hours later the men came back into the bunkhouse and Jess hollered out, "We're hungry. Can't a guy get fed around here?"

Simon came out of the kitchen and replied, "Well then, ring the dinner bell and get all the men in here. I made enough to feed an army and you men don't look like an army to me."

Jess turned and went outside to ring the bell. Within ten minutes, the rest of the hands had arrived. After grace, they all sat down and enjoyed the meal together.

When it was time to leave, John came over and winked at Charity.

"If I wasn't already engaged, I would ask you to be my wife. My mom always told me to marry a woman who can cook and if I only ate your pies, I would be a happy man. Daniel is one lucky man."

Susanna swatted him on his arm saying. "It's a good thing your Bev isn't here to hear that, but I do agree with Simon, they are the flakiest crusts I've ever had."

Charity smiled back at him. "Why thank you, John. No man has ever proposed to me quite that way before. So why didn't you bring your fiancée along?"

"She's a teacher and couldn't get the time off right now."

Daniel had walked over to Charity's side when John had approached her and was grinning.

"I sure am one lucky guy and thank you for noticing." They all laughed and shook hands. "See you Saturday," John reminded.

On Friday afternoon Josh and Vicki arrived.

CHAPTER 24

Cindy arrived Saturday morning around ten to help Charity get the women's menu prepared. They were having small sandwiches and veggies trays to tide them over until the BBQ Simon and his helpers would be making. Joe and his family also arrived around ten; Susanna came inside to help Charity and Cindy while the men went to the barn to set out all the tools and items at different work areas. By noon, people started arriving—they all seemed excited to be there and help Amy and Bruce get ready for their babies. The party had been the talk of the town since they had received their invitations.

Amy and Bruce arrived at half past noon. Bruce laughingly apologized saying, "This beautiful woman just couldn't decide on what to wear! So where do I go?"

Charity grinned. "All men belong in the barn today until the BBQ, when the furniture will be seen by the Mama to be."

Bruce shrugged and turned to his wife. "I'll miss you, sweetheart. I'm being banned to the barn will you miss me?"

"Not on your life, I am so excited I won't even realize you are gone," she said as she kissed him and playfully shoved him out the door.

In the barn Todd was having a great time with the kids and the painting jobs, Daniel kept going back and forth from the furniture-making team to the kid's section so that he and Josiah could do things together. Everyone seemed to be having a good time. Bruce was amazed at the progress the men had already made with the furniture and was eager to jump in and help.

Inside the women were having a great time also. Amy was so pleased with everything, she knew that she wouldn't have to worry about much of anything except how to care for them for quite some time. Her mom and her mother in-law had been seated on either side of her— they too were amazed at the generosity of the women.

By the end of the afternoon, the smells of the BBQ were drawing both the men and women outside. Simon was in his glory ordering men around to get things all ready for this big meal. When everyone was outside, Charity stepped up onto a bench and proclaimed, "Thank you ladies and gentlemen and children for coming today to make this a special day for Bruce and Amy. I'm sure the men won't care what the ladies gave, but I know the women are eager to see what the men have been doing. So Daniel is it ready?"

"Yes it is! Carl would you be so kind as to drive the trailer out here? Bruce, would you please help your wife stand up?"

In a moment, the trailer was visible and then Amy burst into tears. She ran to the trailer and was simply astounded. Bruce helped her get up onto the trailer, and she turned to the crowd tears still falling down her face.

"Never have I felt more loved than just now," Amy wailed. "Thank you everyone for all of this." Amy was lead to the section where the children's activities were on display as the children grabbed their parents to show them what they had done. While they ate, you could still see the shock in Amy's face. Bruce was walking around to everyone thanking him or her personally.

When it was time for dessert, Simon came out of the bunkhouse with two cakes shaped as bassinets—in yellow and green. He had even made the body of a baby inside it with his frosting. Even Charity hadn't known he was that talented. Simon had surprised them all by looking online for the idea.

"This is amazing Simon," Charity whispered.

"I just wanted everything to be perfect for her today," he said, blushing. "She means so much to all of us."

Amy spoke up immediately. "No one is allowed to touch this cake until I get about a hundred pictures of it. Simon, thanks for this beautiful cake to end a perfect day."

After everyone had taken pictures of it, he finally cut it and served them.

Carl drove the trailer to Amy and Bruce's house. Daniel and several other men from the ranch drove over to help unload it. John and Joe were there also, and they all set up the nursery.

"Thank you Charity because I doubt I will have the energy to do anything once I get home."

Charity had smiled. "That's what family and friends are for, you just go home and rest, , we are looking forward to doing this for you."

Susanna and Cindy, Charity and Vicki all arrived right after church then they all went to work putting the nursery together. Amy directed them as to where she would like things as she sat in her rocking chair.

Amy drew Charity aside and told her, "Thank you again for everything you did, I can't believe you did this for me."

"Why wouldn't I, Amy? After all you are my sister now and my best friend."

"Charity, I'm so honored that you feel that way. I'm sorry it wasn't Stephen's baby though."

"Amy, don't ever say that again. I have come to think of Bruce as my other brother. I thought I had made that plain the day you two were married. You are my siblings now."

Amy smiled. "I love you, Charity." "I love you too Amy" and gave her a hug.

Daniel had invited the Casey's to Sunday supper but since the women were busy at Amy's, the guys drove out to the ranch and took a horseback ride first. Josiah was happy that he got to go along. The men got back from their ride just as Charity was giving Sarah her treat since she didn't get to go along. They all went inside to eat then, the talk at dinner was about the party and how fun it had been helping Amy that day.. Everyone was leaving after supper so Charity and Daniel thanked them all as they left for everything they had done to make the party such a success. Carl asked Charity, "Would you mind if I used the pictures I took of the party and use them as a promotion for my business?" "Carl, they are your pictures, you can do whatever you want with them."

Charity sighed once everyone had left. "I don't want to do anything for a few days, this past week has been hectic," she remarked. "How about you Daniel?"

"Me too as I'm sure all the men would agree."

Josiah piped up. "Does that mean I don't go to school tomorrow, Daddy?"

"No son, you'll go to school tomorrow."

"Cool because my friends told me they would see me at school. I like my friends, Daddy."

CHAPTER 25

Monday morning things were back to normal. Daniel drove Josiah to school, and Charity was home busy catching up on her bookwork. Then the phone rang.

"Paradise Ranch. How may I help you?"

"Charity, Pastor Mark here. After you left church yesterday, Mrs. Davis came to me with a little something for you. Can I come out today and deliver it?"

"Sure Pastor, anytime."

"I need to be at Mrs. Bailey's house by eleven, so now would be great."

"Okay, see you soon."

When she heard the doorbell, she knew who it would be. In the meantime, she had made a fresh batch of cinnamon rolls and put on a new pot of coffee. When she opened the door, he smelled them immediately and asked,

"In the kitchen I presume?"

"Yes, sir."

After she poured the coffee and served him a roll, she sat down.

"Charity, Mrs. Davis wanted me to give you this." He handed her the envelope. She opened it up and inside were checks from people in the church.

"What is this for, pastor, I don't understand."

"People wanted to help pay for the materials for the furniture and everything else. They all want to be a part of this," he said and took a bite of the roll. "Oh my, Charity! You have done it again, this roll is divine!"

"Pastor, thank you for the compliment and this envelop. I never expected this, I need to call Virginia and thank her immediately."

"Charity you don't have too, this was a love offering for Amy's party. They all know how tight things are on a rancher's budget and they just wanted to say thank you."

"Pastor, would it be alright if I stood up in church next Sunday and thank everyone for this?"

"I'll write it out so that at second service you could just read it, but do you think they would be upset if I gave some of this to Bruce and Amy?"

"It is yours to do with whatever you want but I'm sure that no one would mind at all," he commented. "May I have another roll? They are just too good to only have one."

"Pastor, why don't you take the rest with you to the Bailey's. I'm sure they would love some too."

"Well then, maybe I'll hold off on another one until I get there. Thank you, Charity."

"Have a good day, Pastor."

She counted it all up when he left—it was well over five hundred dollars. She talked it over with Daniel and they decided to give Bruce and Amy half of it. She had

had a good year due to the dude ranch clients and wanted to share the blessing with others.

Charity stopped by the diner after picking up Josiah from school to drop off the money from the church members. Amy had to sit when she saw what was inside the envelope.

"W-what...what is this Charity?" Amy stammered. "You have already done so much for us."

"This is half of what Mrs. Davis collected from the church members for your party. Pastor Mark said it was to help me pay for the party because they all know how hard it is to make a living ranching, but I just felt that you could use some of this too."

"Oh, Charity! Thank you, this will buy a whole lot of diapers and milk formula, we decided since I'm working at the diner I wouldn't be able to breast-feed them."

"Then could you use the other half? I didn't feel right accepting it since my ranch did very well this year with all the dude ranch clients we had this year."

"No, Charity. You keep the other half. If you don't need it how about dividing up between all the hands, they did so much for us."

"That's a perfect idea, Amy! Thank you."

That evening she discussed it with Daniel and they both agreed that is what they would do with it then. Daniel prayed over the envelope and asked God to bless the money they would give to each hand. Now that things were slowing down a little Daniel and Charity would have more time to spend together getting to know each other better.

Two weeks later the phone rang. "Paradise Ranch. How may I help you?"

It was Bruce. "Charity can you come quickly, Amy just went into labor."

"I'm on my way Bruce. Are you heading off to the hospital right now? Yes, I already called the Doctor he said he'd meet us there."

Charity dialed Daniel's cell and told him she had to leave because Amy's in labor. "I'm going to leave Josiah with Jess and Simon, I'll call you when I know more."

"Drive safely," he said as she was hanging up the phone.

She quickly dialed the bunkhouse to let Simon and Jess know what was going on. Then she hung up and called out to Josiah.

"Josiah, Jess and Simon are coming to watch you, I'm heading to the hospital. Amy's having her babies!"

Jess and Simon came running in; she waved as she was going out the door. "I'll call you when I know something."

She arrived at the hospital an hour later. She found Bruce in the lobby pacing back and forth.

"Charity, I tried, I really tried but they sent me out of the room," he whined. "I fainted twice. Can you go in there and help her?"

"Sure, Bruce, no problem. Which room?"

"The third door down on the left."

An hour later, she told Amy to bear down one more time and out came her first child—a boy. Then a couple of minutes later, another pain came and she bore down again and out came a girl. They washed them up and took care of Amy as Charity quietly walked out of the room looking for Bruce, she found him and a few others in the lobby. They all looked up when she called his name grinning from ear to ear.

"Bruce, you can go in now. Your children are born and they are perfect."

Bruce didn't even wait to hear any more and rushed out of the room to his wife to see his newborn kids. Everyone else asked. "What did they have?"

"A boy and a girl. Does anyone know if he called their folks?"

Pastor Mark answered for the group. "Yes he did, and both said they would leave immediately."

Daniel walked over to Charity. "Are you okay?" he whispered in her ear.

Charity smiled, she loved hearing him ask that question. "I'm fine, thanks for asking." She waited until Bruce came out and then told him, "I need to go do you need anything?"

"No, I'm fine, I'll be staying here tonight with her and the babies. Her folks should arrive tomorrow morning, I should call them and let them know what we had and where I will be," he replied still dazed.

"Bruce, don't worry everything will be alright. Go back to your wife and babies, you can call them from the room."

As they were driving home, Charity asked Daniel if he wanted more children. She blushed as she asked. Daniel pulled over to the side of the road, pulled her into his arms.

"Charity whatever God decides, I'll be happy with it. I hope you can say the same thing."

"Yes, Daniel. Whatever God desires I'll go along with."

He then pulled back onto the road and they continued driving home, but she stayed right next to his side. The next morning Charity called the hospital to find out that Amy and the babies had just left for home.

October and November just flew by, Charity and Daniel learned more of each other, every Friday night one of the ranch hands would take a turn babysitting Josiah so that they could go out on a date. Charity enjoyed their adult time together but realized that she loved Josiah as much as his father and decided she didn't want to leave him home every week. So twice a month they made their date on a Saturday and included activities that Josiah would enjoy also. Cindy and Joe began dating after the party and sometimes they even double dated with them.

On December 1, Cindy called and told Charity the good news.

"Joe proposed! Have you set your date yet?"

"Yes, Daniel and I finally agreed on a date, June 25. That way school will be out and Josh and Vicki can babysit while we are on our honeymoon. We just want a small, intimate wedding."

"Charity, by small do you mean just church members? You know that you won't be able to get away with anything smaller than the whole church but I doubt the town would agree to that either."

"I know but I could dream, couldn't I?"

"You can but I doubt that is going to happen."

"Congratulations, Cindy! I wish you and Joe all the best. However, you don't need to wait until after ours if you don't want to. When were you thinking, Cindy"

"Well…" she paused. "Joe mentioned something about the end of August, that is his vacation time, so I guess it will be around then."

"That means we will be busy this winter helping each other plan our weddings then, won't we? Have you told his folks yet?"

"Yes. we called them last night after he gave me the ring, then we told my folks when he took me home."

"Thank you, Charity, for introducing us."

"Cindy you arranged that, I didn't really do anything."

"Yes, we both know that but he thinks it was all you."

"Aren't you going to tell him?"

"Do I have to?"

"Yes, you need to be honest with him from the start."

Cindy sighed heavily. "Okay if I must, I must"

"Don't worry, Cindy I don't think it will make one bit of difference to him."

Just as she hung up the phone it rang again.

"Paradise Ranch. How may I help you?"

"Charity, it's Amy have you heard? Cindy is engaged. Joe was just in the diner and told us."

"Yes I have I just hung up with her. They set their date for the end of August"

"Have you and Daniel finally set a date?"

"Yes. We agreed on the twenty-fifth of June, that way school is over and Vicki and Josh can babysit Josiah while we are on our honeymoon."

"Good idea, Charity. I want to help you as much as I can."

"Amy, believe me, I plan on asking for a lot of help, and Cindy informed me when I told her I wanted a small wedding that she doubted the town would allow that."

"Oh, Bruce is here. I've gotta go now but just wanted to make sure you knew, I told you that love was in the air, didn't I?"

"Yes you did, Amy. Give my love to Bruce."

At dinner Charity told Daniel about Joe and Cindy.

"I know," he replied, "Joe told me this morning when I dropped Josiah off at school."

CHAPTER 26

Charity Daniel and Josiah had chopped down their Christmas tree on Thanksgiving weekend. However, Charity had explained that her parents always told her that you have to let the limbs settle a week before decorating it. Charity and Josiah had already started making paper chains after school. Josiah made a star for the top and covered it in foil during class. Daniel looked lovingly into her eyes as her proclaimed , I *never* would have thought that you would be happy with a child's tree." "Wait until you see our family decorations, I doubt you will think that then." When Daniel brought the boxes marked Christmas down from the attic, she opened them up lovingly and showed off all her treasures. "My mother has saved every ornament we had made throughout our school years, and I think there are even some that my parents made in here.

This is how I was raised and I want to continue that tradition," Charity said thoughtfully.

Daniel took her in his arms. "John was right. I am the luckiest man on earth."

"Daniel, I'm so glad Vicki and Josh are coming for Christmas, the house will be full. Speaking of full, I need to go Christmas shopping."

"How do you get to, I need to go Christmas shopping, from full?"

"Easy, Daniel. Stockings"

"Oh I get it, so are you asking if we can go shopping this weekend?"

"Yes. You and Josiah can go off on your own, and I will do my shopping, then we meet at one for lunch then it's my turn to take Josiah with me and you get to go alone."

"Sounds like a good plan to me. This Saturday is our Josiah date day anyway."

After shopping all day long, they came home, hid their presents, and started to decorate the tree. Josiah was so wound up he was chatting everyone's head off.

Charity thought, *oh this reminds me so much of my parents, except I was the chatterbox.* Jess and Simon had volunteered to help decorate and keep an eye on Josiah while Daniel popped the corn and Charity strung it.

"Anyone want hot chocolate?" Simon asked.

They all wanted some so he went to make it. When the tree was almost finished, Daniel lifted Josiah up to place the star on the top.

Charity happily sighed. "Jess don't you think this is the best tree we've had."

He smiled right back at her. "Just like always, only it gets better every year."

Josiah yawned just then and Charity noticed. "Daniel I think someone is sleepy, he's had a very long day."

Josiah heard it, and so he exclaimed, "No I'm not!"

They all laughed and Jess answered back, "Well I am. Good night everyone." Off they went to the bunkhouse.

Daniel turned to his son. "Well I am too, so it's time we leave ourselves, son."

"Aw, dad! Do we have to? I want to fall asleep right here under this bestest tree ever."

"Yes we have to, son. Come on, I will give you a horsey ride home."

"Dad, it's called a piggy back ride, Danny told me. He says that is what his dad calls it."

"Okay son, when did you get so smart?"

"I have always been smart, Dad. You just didn't know it yet."

Charity couldn't help it, she burst out laughing. "And with that my two men, I will say good night to you!"

Once they had gone, Charity got out her wrapping paper and began wrapping her gifts.

Christmas vacation…what wonderful memories I have of them, Charity thought. B*aking with mom, riding with dad, and just sitting by the fire and playing games with the family. I hope my life with Daniel and Josiah will be the same.*

Just then Daniel walked in. "Are you all right?" he asks.

Charity smiled. "Yes, I am. Why?" she replied. "I just felt like you needed me."

"I do need you, Daniel. Thank you for coming. I'm sitting here, reflecting on past Christmases and wondering if you and I will have the same kind with Josiah."

He walked over to her, pulled her out of the chair and hugged her. "Charity I hope that you know I want to do everything in my power to make you happy. What can I do, sweetheart?"

"Nothing more than what you are right now, loving."

"Is that all, I can do more if you want."

"Daniel, all I need is your love. That's what I was thinking about, I miss my family but what I really miss is all the things we did, mostly just the love we had for one another."

"Charity I promise you that we will have the love. Josiah already loves you, and you know I do. He prayed last night that you would be his mother so he could take you to show and tell."

"Oh, Daniel! That is so sweet, do we have to wait until June? I don't think they have show and tell in first grade."

Daniel cupped her face in his hands. "Honey we can get married anytime you like." "Then how about tomorrow?"

"Not on your life, everyone in this town would be mad at me."

"I don't care about them. I want Josiah to be my son just as much as he wants me to be his mommy."

"Charity you already are, just not in name. He comes to you for everything."

Charity smiled sweetly. "But I want to walk down the hall and peek in and see his angelic face sleeping."

"You will honey you will."

He couldn't help it, he just lowered his head to kiss those sweet pouting lips.

Charity put her head on his shoulders and sighed, as if coming home.

❧

Soon school was out for the holidays, and then it was Christmas Eve. Vicki and Josh arrived just after two o'clock in the afternoon. Dinner was going to be early so that everyone could attend the Christmas Eve service at church. Josiah was a shepherd in the children's skit, and Daniel and Charity were singing a duet as Mary and Joseph for the adult skit.

Josiah came running into the house on Christmas morning to wake everyone up.

"Grandma, Grandpa," he shouted as he shook them, "get up Santa's been here!" He then went to the next room. "Charity come quick, Santa filled our stockings." Then he ran downstairs. "Daddy look!"

He was so excited. Slowly (according to Josiah) the adults appeared downstairs, the coffee pot had been set and now the smell of fresh coffee was greeting them. Charity went into the kitchen and brought out a tray of coffee and cups. Josiah was impatiently waiting for them to sit so he could open his stocking. After the stockings, Josiah turned to his dad.

"Is it time yet, I've been waiting forever"

Daniel just shrugged. "That's up to everyone else. Are you guys all ready?" he asked.

"Come on Daniel don't keep the kid waiting any longer," Josh spoke up. "Can't you see he is busting his seams he's so eager?"

Daniel laughed. "Yes, but first things first, a sip of coffee. Okay son you may now pass out the presents."

"Yippee!" Since Josiah had the most gifts he opened a present after each adult opened one.

When they had opened their presents, they all sat down to breakfast.

"Josiah it's time we go deliver our presents to the men," Daniel announced. "Are you ready?"

"Yes, I am. Come on everyone, you have to go with us." He picked up an apple as he went out the door. "I'll be right back, Dad. I have to say good morning to Star."

"Wait for me I need to do the same to Sarah," Charity called out and grabbed a couple of sugar cubes and they held hands as they walked to the barn.

They cut the apple in half, and Charity gave him half her sugar cubes.

"This way we are both giving something to each animal Josiah."

After they talked to and fed their horses, they skipped over to the bunkhouse. Josiah came in the door. "You didn't start yet did you, Dad? I want to see it all."

It was Simon who replied though. "I was just telling them I couldn't wait for you two horse lovers anymore. You got here just in the nick of time, a minute later and you would have missed out."

"No sir," Jess harrumphed. "I wouldn't let you do that, Simon."

All the men laughed.

"Okay you two this is Christmas Day quit your harping and let's get this thing started," Todd said.

Daniel and Charity handed out their gifts to the men. Josiah got one from Jess, Simon, and one from the hands also. Simon provided prime rib for Christmas Dinner while Charity cooked a turkey. Charity thought to herself, *ah family and friends, just as it should be on this wondrous day.*

Josh and Vicki stayed until after the New Year so that Daniel and Vicki could go to Scott and Sophia's New Year's Eve party with all her friends. At the stroke of midnight, Daniel kissed her and whispered, "Happy

New Year Honey! I can't wait until next year when you are really mine." "Me too," Charity responded, "but I am yours already."

Daniel kissed her again.

January rolled into February, one day the phone rang and Charity answered it.

"Paradise Ranch. How may I help you?"

"Charity, it's Cindy. I thought I would let you know ASAP. Jimmy was just in the store, he was asking how you were."

She shuddered and gasped out, "What did you tell him?"

"That you were engaged is all."

"Okay, thanks for the advance notice Cindy I appreciate it."

As she hung up she was stunned. *Why would he ask about me*, she thought. Just then the phone rang again.

"Paradise Ranch. How may I help you?"

CHAPTER 28

"Charity, it's Jimmy. I- I…I want to apologize to you. Can we meet at the diner?"

"Why Jimmy?"

"Because I treated you badly and I would like, well I want your forgiveness."

"Jimmy that isn't necessary, I have forgiven you and God has brought someone new into my life. I am engaged to Daniel and I'm very happy. We were young and neither of us were ready to make that step, I realize that now."

"Charity, Lucy and I broke up. Well actually, she left me for another man. That started me thinking how badly I treated you."

"No need Jimmy I've recovered from that now and I wish you all the best. I'm sorry that it didn't work out for you and Lucy though. Are you just passing through or are you going to move back here?"

"I'm actually hoping to find some work in town and get a place to stay. I feel drawn to this place for some reason. Thank you for your forgiveness, it means a lot to me Charity."

"Jimmy, I must confess it took a long time for me to be able to forgive anyone. I turned away from God and my faith, but eventually God broke me and I asked his forgiveness. I hope you do, too. I truly hope that you can find happiness just as I have."

"Charity, I need to tell you that when Lucy left me I lost it. I met a woman, she and I started going to church together, I'm walking with God now too and that's why I had to ask you for your forgiveness. Her name is Mary, and we are engaged to be married. I feel drawn to here and want to settle here if you don't mind?"

"Mind? Jimmy if you feel God is leading you then you have to do it."

"Thanks Charity and by the way congratulations. Have you set your date yet?" Yes we have, it's in June, have you and Mary set a date?"

"Mary wants to be married in the church here. We came this weekend to talk to Pastor Mark." "Oh, Jimmy! I'm so happy for you. God has truly blessed us both in spite of us trying to do things our way."

Just then, Daniel walked in and overheard her conversation. When he heard the name Jimmy, he was ready to protect Charity. However, he could see that she wasn't having any trouble speaking to him—she looked happy in fact. He walked over to her and she hugged him. She looked up at him smiling as she asked, "Jimmy would you and Mary like to come here for dinner tonight? I would like to meet her."

"Really Charity? Hold on and let me ask her." "Sure," she said.

Jimmy turned to Mary who was standing beside him. "Mary, Charity just invited us to dinner, would you like to accept?"

"Jimmy, it's up to you, are you sure?" his fiancée said.

"Yes Mary, I'm sure Charity is sincere."

"Then yes, I would like to accept." Mary put an arm around Jimmy's waist as he relayed her answer to Charity.

"Charity she said yes, what time?"

"How about six o'clock?" Charity gazed adoringly into Daniel's eye as she told Jimmy the time to arrive.

"Perfect, see you then." Daniel gave her a questioning look as she said that.

"Are you sure about this, after what he did to you?"

"Yes, Daniel. I'm sure, he asked for my forgiveness and I gave it to him. What better way to show that?"

At quarter to six, Jimmy and Mary rang the doorbell. When Charity opened the door, the first thing she noticed was how much he had changed. He looked happy and contented; Charity couldn't remember him looking that way when they were going out.

Thank you Lord for not allowing us to make a mistake so long ago, Charity prayed. She ushered them in and introduced them to Daniel, her fiancé.

Jess came in just then and so Charity introduced Mary to him. She had gone to talk to Jess after her call with Jimmy earlier. Jess was cautious, and Daniel wouldn't leave her side—Charity had never felt so loved. During dinner, they discussed the ranch and Jimmy was impressed what the men had done.

"Oh, Charity you are so blessed to have such a loving family."

She smiled back to Jimmy and replied, "Yes I am and as I told you over the phone earlier, I am so thankful. I hope you two find a place you like and you find a job. This town is a wonderful place to live in. I know just how you feel, Jimmy. This town just draws you to it."

She turned to Mary. "So Mary, how did you like Pastor Mark?"

"Oh he seemed so nice, he invited us to stay at his house this weekend and said he would put the word out that Jimmy was looking for a job."

"So will you be looking for a job also?"

"Yes, I will apply at the hospital. I met Nancy a couple of years ago at a physical therapists conference, and she said then that they seem to always be in need of one, if Jimmy finds a job then I will apply."

"Nancy was my therapist, and I am so thankful that she was, she does a tremendous job. I hope you two find your niche here, Mary."

"Thank you, Charity. Jimmy was hesitant about coming back here because of what he had done but I told him to face up to it and move on with his life. He talks about this community all the time but was afraid. I repeatedly had to remind him that God is not a God of fear, once you confess your sin it is forgotten. He just wasn't ready to forgive himself until now."

"Oh, Mary! How true that is! I, too, struggled with forgiveness but God persisted and finally I broke down and repented, when I did things just got better. Each new day holds hope and a promise of joy if only we are willing to accept it."

Mary smiled. "You do live up to your name I hope we can become good friends."

"Me too, Mary"

Jimmy and Daniel hit it off too. Daniel admitted to Charity later that evening that at first he still wanted to hurt him but by the end of the evening he had passed that and he found that he actually liked him.

Sunday morning after church, Mary came up to Charity and told her that Jimmy had found a job, so they would be moving here.

"Tomorrow I am going to the hospital to apply then we'll go back home and start packing our things. Nancy told us that she would look for an apartment for Jimmy but that I could rent a room from them. I'm so happy"

"Mary that's great. Oh I want you to meet a couple of my friends, Cindy and Amy."

As the four men walked up, they heard the women all laughing at something. Daniel remarked that it was good to know they were happy.

The men all nodded and agreed, seems as if they all had made some new friends.

CHAPTER 29

The warden had finally given Nathaniel his notice of his release date; he was feverishly working to finish his studies before then. His mother came every week to visit him and this Saturday his Dad was coming along with her. She indicated that his father had something important to tell him. However, when he asked her what, she just told him to wait until they came. All that week Nathaniel pondered what his father would have to say. He remembered the trial, and what his father had said at that time and hoped he had forgiven him finally.

He had said, "Son I am embarrassed to be seen in this city after what you did. How could you do this to your mother and me? We didn't raise you to do this to us. I hope they send you to jail for life, I don't want to see you ever again. Even though Chris Stewart wasn't my friend, he was an acquaintance, and I am ashamed to call you my son."

Even now just reliving that moment was so painful for Nathaniel, just at the time when he needed his father the most he had rebuked him, told him he wished that he had never been born and walked out. The moment his father said that, he broke down and sobbed. He realized just then exactly what he had done, killed his best friend and his parents, maimed Charity, alienated himself from his own family and broke his grandmother's heart. That was the moment he called out to God and asked for forgiveness. From that moment on, he dedicated his life to God and his service.

Saturday he awoke feeling trepidation. *What will my dad have to say? Do I really want to know, will he hurt me more or has he come to forgive me? Just another couple of hours and I will know. Please Lord, let him forgive me, and if possible that he has decided to follow you also.* Two o'clock was nearing, he prayed constantly for comfort.

When his name was called, telling him his visitors were being seated, he straightened his shoulders and walked out the door to the visiting room. He cautiously looked over to where his father sat. His father actually smiled at him.

This may go better than I was hoping, he thought. As he greeted them, his father started his speech without further ado.

"Son...I- I need to apologize to you. This has been brewing in me for a long time now, and I can't hold it in anymore. Please forgive me for all those ugly things I said to you during the trial. You are my son and even though what you did caused harm, I never meant what I said. I never really wished you weren't born. I love you, son. Will you forgive me?"

"Father, of course I forgive you." Nathaniel was in tears. "How could you think I wouldn't? I'm sure mother has told you all about what I've been doing since I've been here. I've dedicated my life to serving God, not out of penance but because he forgave me. How could I not forgive you?"

"Son, thank you. Do you know that I see my mother in you? I have even noticed a difference in your mother too since she started attending church with my mom. I want that peace, how do you get it?"

"You trust in God, Dad, and that's it. You live by his word and accept him into your heart."

That day instead of just a visit from his folks, he led his father to God.

Their visiting hour was up. His father asked if he could come back tomorrow so they could actually visit, he wanted to talk to him more.

"I'd love it, Dad," Nathaniel said.

That night he slept peacefully. The next day just his father returned, his father told him his mother went to church with his grandmother.

"Son tell me all about your time here. What you have done. I've missed you so much." Nathaniel tried to tell him as much as he could within the allotted visiting time. It felt good to know that his father would acknowledge him again. He also talked to his dad about attending church with his mother.

"Grandma has been praying for you and mom for years, Dad. Why not go and just listen with an open heart to Pastor Mark. He's a nice guy, Dad. You would like him."

As his father left that day, he told him that he would be back the next Saturday, along with his mother.

"I guess I'll go meet this Pastor Mark and listen to what he has to say for once."

"Dad did you know Grandma comes every Sunday to visit, if you want you could come too."

"Maybe I will son, maybe I will."

Nathaniel saw Pastor Mark after his father left and relayed everything that had happened.

"Do you think he would mind if I called on him at his house this week, Nathaniel?" "Pastor Mark, I think that now he wouldn't mind at all."

Wednesday morning Pastor Mark stopped at the Davis' house, Mrs. Davis invited him in and called out to her husband.

"We have a visitor."

He was introduced to the Pastor as he walked into the living room.

"Nice to meet you finally, Mr. Davis. Your mother and Nathaniel have mentioned you several times. Your mother asked me yesterday at the meeting to stop by today and introduce myself."

"Yes my mother can be intimidating at times. My name is Gordon by the way, nice to meet you pastor."

They visited for half an hour or so, and Mr. Davis promised that he would be there Sunday morning with his wife and mother.

That Sunday morning Charity saw Mrs. Davis in her normal pew towards the front, and sitting right next to her was her son and daughter in-law. She went over to say *good morning* to them before she went to the choir room. As she was leaving, she saw Simon and Jess and pointed in Mrs. Davis's direction so they could go greet them also. They both walked over and Virginia introduced her son to them. She invited them to sit in the pew with them, Simon ended up on her other side. Jess smiled, *so Simon really does like Virginia as much as she likes him.*

After church service, Charity brought Daniel over to greet them also.

CHAPTER 30

The next few months seemed to fly by. The three couples were busy planning their weddings. One day Charity was upstairs in the attic and opened up a trunk of her mother's, inside it was her wedding dress. Charity couldn't help herself, she had to try it on. It fit perfectly and decided immediately that she would wear it for her wedding also. She called Amy immediately and told her.

"Oh, Charity that is perfect!" Amy exclaimed. She had asked Amy to be her maid of honor, they both decided that Amy should wear Charity's senior prom dress that her father had thought was a wedding dress as a way to have her parents a part of the ceremony.

One day, Simon pulled Charity aside and asked if he could speak with her privately.

Charity thought to herself, *I hope he doesn't want to retire like Jess. I couldn't make it without him.*

Still, she agreed to meet with him later that day. Simon was playing chess with Jess when she arrived for their talk. Jess was about ready to excuse him when Simon told him, "You don't need to leave, this concerns you too." He looked directly into Charity's eyes. "Charity, love is in the air, I seem to recall hearing that somewhere"

"Yes, Simon. I did say that but I'm hoping it doesn't mean what I think it does."

"Well now, yes and no Charity. I seem to have been bitten by the same bug. However, I've no intention of retiring, so don't fret about that. Since you and Daniel are getting married soon, I was wondering if Jess could take over his rooms again. I'm going to ask Virginia to marry me. We could live at her place as I'm sure she wouldn't want to live here, but I would still come to work."

"Simon, have you spoken to her about it yet, is that what she wants?"

"Yes I have, Charity, but we haven't worked out any details yet, so maybe this talk is premature."

"I saw this coming and have been thinking on it," Jess spoke. "I would like to take over my old rooms, but maybe Simon it's time for you to retire. I'm sure that you think you would still come to work here but that isn't fair to Virginia. My nephew Jason, who just graduated from a chef's school would jump at the chance to work here. I could call him if you like. He can live in Josiah's room and keep me company and you and Virginia can just enjoy yourselves."

"Let's pray about this before we do anything but I've noticed a glow on Mrs. Davis' face at our meetings recently," Charity told them both. "Hiring a new chef could be a good idea. I've haven't been fair to you Simon, just as I never thought to hire someone to replace Jess.

You two are family to me, so I never wanted you two to leave me."

"Charity, I would still be around for you, you know that don't you?" Simon said.

"Yes, Simon. I know that, thank you both for caring so much about me. Let's pray about it and say meet a week from today?"

During that week Charity prayed about it, spoke to Mrs. Davis, called Jess's nephew, and prayed some more. When the day arrived of their meeting, Charity was at peace. She had already invited Jason to come see the ranch and to learn the ropes from Simon if he liked it there. Simon had discussed things with Virginia, and she agreed with his decision—they would never be too far from Charity but things were changing. Jess was looking forward to having his nephew Jason arrive. Therefore, they all sat down and agreed that this change was for the best.

Jason arrived a week after the meeting, he seemed to fall in love with the place instantly. Charity was impressed at his culinary knowledge. *He could even become a better chef than Simon*, she thought, *which would benefit the ranch*. At the same time, she looked over at Jess and wanted him to find love also. Jess had begun to think about his family more and more and had been praying that more than just his nephew Jason would move here.

Charity still served on the Prison Bible Study committee and one day while they were there Nathaniel told her some good news.

"I've gotten my release date it's the fourteenth of May. I'm so excited."

"Oh, Nathaniel congratulations! Your mother will be so excited to have you back home."

"I know I can't wait, Grandma is so excited, then her whole family will be attending that little church together for the first time."

Charity went home and told Daniel the good news. "I already know, Jimmy told me last Sunday. He said he had asked if Nathaniel would be his best man. But I get to throw the bachelor party."

Charity smiled. "Oh really? Do you plan on having a bachelor party also?"

Daniel laughed. "Of course, My best man will see to that."

"Daniel you haven't told me yet whom you chose as your best man. Amy needs to know."

"Amy needs to know or you do?"

"Okay then fine, I want to know."

"It's Josiah."

Charity smiled. "That's perfect, Daniel"

"Well I figured that you would ask Jess to walk you down the aisle, so I couldn't ask him even though he was the one who hired me so we could meet. You did ask Jess didn't you Charity?"

"Yes the morning after you gave me the ring."

With only two weeks until her wedding Charity was getting nervous. Going round and round in her head were these thoughts. *Would Amy's dress still fit now that she was pregnant again? Would Simon be able to handle the reception? What if Nathaniel didn't pass his exam?*

Thankfully, Nathaniel called her the next day happily proclaiming the good news.

"I passed! Now I can officiate your wedding. Let me tell you I was nervous, I've never wanted anything as much as passing this exam."

Charity sighed and sent up a prayer, *thank you Lord.*

The next week they had their final fittings, and the dressmaker declared that no changes were necessary on Amy's dress. Simon came to her the day after and told her, "Don't worry I hired extra help for the reception so that I can still be at your ceremony."

Vicki and Josh showed up a day early just to ease Charity's mind about them making it there on time. Everything seemed to be going as planned.

The morning of her wedding she was unusually calm. She looked up towards heaven and spoke to her folks. "I am marrying Daniel today. Thank you for all you have done to prepare me." A single tear rolled down her face.

As she started down the aisle, the sun broke through the clouds and a bright ray shone through the window unto the glowing bride. Daniel noticed it first and sent up a silent thank you as he watched her walk towards him. "Help me to love and honor this woman you have given me Lord," he whispered. The church bell rang as the happy couple exited the church.

Two weeks later, they returned from their honeymoon trip. Josiah was now calling her mommy and Charity felt so blessed. Vicki and Josh had decided to move to town to be closer to them. They arrive today.

I need to get moving so I can be at their new house waiting for them, Charity thought. She stretched and got up and dressed. Before anything though she peeped into Josiah's room to see if he was awake, he was dressing himself and looked when the door opened.

"Mom, do we have time to go see our horses before we have to leave for Grandma and Grandpa's house?"

"Of course we do, sweetie," Charity said. "In fact, we can even take a short ride before we have breakfast. How does that sound?"

"Cool! I'd love that, Mom!"

Charity had to smile because Josiah was exactly like her. After their short ride, they brushed down their horses and went to the bunkhouse for some grub. Josiah loved eating at the bunkhouse. One time she asked him about it.

"Why not our kitchen?"

"Because I'm a cowboy mom," he told her. "I have to eat here."

Simon and his protégé Jason, seemed to think so, too.

At around noon, they arrived at Josh and Vicki's new house. Josiah jumped out of the truck and ran to open the door. "What time are they coming, Mom?"

Daniel replied instead. "Slow down, son. No need to run, they aren't coming for a few more minutes."

Just then, Josh pulled the moving truck into the driveway with Vicki right behind him in their car.

"Wow, Dad! We made it just in time," Josiah blurted.

"Looks like it, son. I told you we didn't need to hurry."

"But Dad we had the key I just had to be here before them, otherwise how would they have got in?"

Charity knelt down and held Josiah's tiny face. "God never lets us be late for something so important, don't ever forget that."

"Yes, Mom!"

Vicki got out of the car first. "Josh wanted to leave a day early. He couldn't wait to get here, but for some reason the car had a flat that day so we couldn't."

"Good thing you didn't because Josiah wanted to be the one to give you the key to your new house," Charity happily said.

"Grandma come on! Let' go see inside, Mom got you a present."

Vicki looked at her and smiled. "Doesn't that sound nice? Okay let me in then, honey."

As they entered their house, they were meet by the smell of cinnamon.

"Come on, Grandma. I can't have one until you do, so hurry I can't wait any longer."

Charity laughed out loud. "You should have heard him on the drive over here, trying to get me to give him one but Daniel sternly said no."

Vicki smiled. "I don't blame him because they are so good. Come on Josiah, I'll share one with you."

"Share? Aw.......do I have to, I'm a growing boy and need a whole one!"

Vicki grinned, "Too big to hold Grandmas hand?"
"Josiah put a finger on his cheek as he thought about that, "No, come on grandma give me your hand, I'm starving." Off they went to the kitchen. Josiah skipped because he was so happy they had finally arrived.

Vicki and Josh soon ensconced themselves into the community. She joined several committees and Josh volunteered to build a gazebo in the town's square park. Turns out he recruited several men to help him: Daniel, Joe, Jimmy, and Bruce. Charity and Vicki were in town shopping and stopped by, to her surprise she saw Carl and John too. Carl winked when he saw her.

"John's fiancée wants to have their wedding under a gazebo. So when Joe told us about Josh wanting to build one, John and I offered to assist them if they could have the wedding here Joe got the final okay from the mayor last week, so here we are."

John walked over to Charity and said, "Oh by the way, I want you to meet my fiancée Bev."

"Beverly, this is Charity."

"Charity, it's so nice to finally meet you," Bev said. "We used your idea for my sister's baby shower and the whole town had a wonderful time! What a great idea that was."

"Well once I got the idea it just seemed to grow bigger every time we discussed something. I'm glad to meet you, too. John mentioned you several times that day."

That evening everyone came out to the ranch for an impromptu BBQ. Susanna had told Bev all about the place, and she was eagerly looking forward to seeing it.

Simon was in his element, Jason was almost ready to be on his own and then he and Virginia could relax and allow their relationship to bloom even more than it already had. They had a group of clients that week, so when Charity called about having a BBQ he quickly agreed. Today was their first day of riding the fence line and making repairs, so he knew they would enjoy a little fun that evening.

Beverly explained to both Daniel and Charity that her family were farmers and were interested in hearing more about her ranch. Daniel and some of the men sat down to think about how they could tweak it to work for a farm also. Helping each other seemed to come naturally to the group. Charity sat back and thought, *thank you Lord!*

Beverly had mentioned that her grandmother would be arriving tomorrow for Joe's wedding because she wanted to see the gazebo.

"Grandma and Grandpa were married in one, which is where I got the idea. Now that Grandpa is dead, Grandma has been traveling a lot. She said they never got the chance to travel much working on the farm."

Much to Charity's surprise, Beverly's grandmother came to the wedding rehearsal and for some reason, Joe had asked Jess to come also. *Maybe Jess will find love too*, Charity thought as she watched them talking together the whole evening. That brought to mind the scene from the other night, the one where Jess had read the letter from Doug and his niece Katrina. They had decided to move their dental practice office here so they could raise their children in a small town environment. Charity recalled how his eyes had sparkled as he read it aloud to everyone. Jason had added that his mom had mentioned in her letter to him that even she was thinking of moving here.

Two days later was Joe and Cindy's wedding. Once again, Charity and Daniel were standing up in front of the church, this time though as matron of honor and best man. Charity blushed as she looked over at Daniel during the ceremony. She had some news she needed to tell him. Daniel caught her blushing and wondered why. During the reception, he leaned over and asked her why she was blushing during the ceremony.

She leaned closer. "I have something to tell you."

He stared at her. "Are you pregnant?"

"How did you know?"

"I didn't, you just told me. And did you know your face glows?"

"Yes, I noticed this morning. Are you happy?"

"You just made me happier than I could imagine."

"No Daniel you have made me the happiest person! You brought me love, God, a son, and now another child on the way."

ABOUT
CAROL L. CURTIS

Ms. Curtis is native to Southern California, except for her high school years when she lived in Spokane Washington. She has read romance books all her life. After thirty years of working in an office for a contractor, she decided to venture out and change her career direction with something very different. She is dedicating this first book to her mother for her support during this time and Derek for his encouragement, to both of you. I say a heartfelt thank you.